Teenage Hobo

Teenage Hobo

MY BROTHERS KEEPER

Robert S. Weil

To order additional copies of this book, contact:
Xlibris Corporation
1-888-795-4274
www.Xlibris.com
Orders@Xlibris.com
102810

Contents

Dedication

To my brothers Jack and David, as well as to Jim, who have provided me the faith and reliance needed during the days of trial. My thanks are forever to them and to the angel that certainly looked after us.

Introduction

The growth of mankind through the ages has often resulted in man facing a fine edge of survival. Survival is finally dependent upon a critical development of self-reliance within each individual.

Birth breathes the gamble of life into the newborn babes. Many variables will be introduced during the ages of these new lives. Each variable in itself may alter the lives' progress. The life will grow with glorious advances or collapse within itself, dependent on the individual's self-reliance or fortitude.

Fortitude, as defined in my dictionary, is an inner strength which is an inherited characteristic. Humans have developed methods of enhancing each individual's fortitude. Some methods are by repetitive training and examples of others' experiences. It is those experiences that awaken the fortitude within a person. Self reliance oftentimes shows itself with electrifying results.

Countless people have walked the face of this earth, adding small changes to life's style of living. The experiences of each human have been the mold of mankind's evolution.

The evolution of fortitude has become the fine edge that young people usually find themselves balancing upon. Some young people are not able to maintain themselves and, therefore, do not survive.

Other young people are able to broaden their gifted talent. It is these young people whose fortitude enables them to survive, to advance mankind's evolution of experiences.

Survival is by no means a simple result of living. There are many storms faced by each person with the breath of life. People find they must survive minor difficulties as well as catastrophic calamities—both as vital and most important as a small child's tear.

How can people recognize the fortitude in others? Ask a young person how he or she would handle some holocaust that they may face. Observe this young person carefully; note the strength in the answer, if they can answer at all. Recognize the evolutionary fortitude that does or does not demonstrate his or her wise counsel.

Wise counsel, strength of action, and survival in the period of disasters are all ageless. It does not require a genius or a wise elder to understand the art of survival.

Three young boys found life thrusting the need of survival during difficult experiences, which people twenty or thirty years older may never face. The experiences they faced daily were unexpected and extremely hazardous. Each event could have resulted in their conquest or end of life. The ages in development of life's fortitude were with these boys.

Two of these boys were my younger brothers: Jack and David. I was the ripe old age of fourteen at the time the events took place during the summer of 1941. Jack was two years younger, twelve. David was exactly four years younger than I, ten. David had been born on my birthday, as I had been born on our dad's birthday.

I do not reflect back on this time with any form of nostalgia. On the contrary, as each of the days are recalled, I cannot remember a single day that was a full day of pleasantries.

Each day into the trip began with a fog of apprehension, obscuring any warmth of the morning sunrise. For about thirty days, this apprehension was repeated. The exhausting trudge of walking alongside many miles of highways. The fear of what might occur while riding within noisy freight train boxcars. The wonder if we would indeed make the thousands of miles to our goal of rejoining our unknowing mother in Los Angeles. All these periods of concern would be with me. I would hope I would be able to conceal these feelings from my brothers. I knew they too must be exhausted, but we had to move on; we had to succeed. I also knew Mother would be angry when she found out about what we had done. She would not be mad. Dogs get mad; people get angry.

Traveling was a state of mind that developed into zombielike paralysis. There were fabulous wonders to be seen, but as the many people before, struggling in their own time of travels, these splendors were lost in the exhausting daily misery.

The emotions of young people, as we were, did contain periods of fear and painful discomfort. As time rolled by, the world began to appear to pass in slow motion. I felt we were not of the same world that we were dragging ourselves through. I wondered if this was my punishment in hell for the many wrong deeds in my past. If so, why were my brothers being subjected to this same misery?

Chapter 1

FREIGHTER FRIGHT

"Please, God, don't let me lose my little brother after we've made it this far," I fervently prayed.

The train had lurched forward suddenly when it changed gears for the power necessary to continue its struggle up the precipitous incline. Little David, caught off guard, was thrown off balance. As I braced myself, I caught a glimpse of him in my peripheral vision. It looked as though he were about to fall forward and fly straight out the open door. And then all I could see was the terrifying emptiness between the tracks and the floor of the yawning canyon hundreds of feet below.

David gasped in fright just as Jack and I jerked around to see him seem to fall in slow motion. As he was falling across our laps, we automatically grabbed frantically for any part of David we could catch and just barely managed to drag him back into the safety of the freight car, away from the gaping door through which he'd been heading.

We all broke out in a cold sweat when we became fully aware of the horror that had nearly happened to us. Jack was as white as a ghost, and David gave a little laugh to cover his fright.

"G-g-g-gee, th-th-that was cl-close," I could hear myself stammer in a hoarse, barely audible voice. We quickly moved to the back of the car, as far away from the open door as possible. And that's where we stayed for the rest of that nerve-racking ride.

It took me a long, long time to get to sleep that night. Our recent misadventures had been teaching us many lessons, and I lay awake for ages thinking about the one we'd learned tonight. To survive in this world, we must always be on the alert for the many unsuspected hazards that seem to be everywhere. Tonight's lesson had come cheap, compared to how dear a price we had almost had to pay. The thought of that cost made me shudder as I lay awake next to my sleeping brothers: twelve-year-old Jack, two years younger than me and ten-year-old David.

As I lay there listening to the clickety-clack of the train's wheels, the events of the last few months replayed themselves in my mind. And as I got sleepier and sleepier, it seemed as though the whole thing had been a dream—just a bad dream that I was still having. How did we ever get into this position?

"Will I ever get home in this dream and wake up?" I asked myself.

Chapter 2

THE JOURNEY TO CINCINNATI

Our loss had been sudden—unbelievable. One moment we had been a big happy family comprised of a warm and beautiful mother, a hardworking and loving father, one pretty girl, five rambunctious boys, and from time to time, our Uncle Rob. The next moment, our lives were shattered like fine china would be if dropped from a skyscraper onto the sidewalks of Los Angeles. The family's path would now follow a different route than the one that had been anticipated. My mother was forced to completely give up the beautiful plans she had and draft new expectations and hopes.

During the time of the Great Depression, the American people suddenly found themselves in financial bankruptcy. Almost overnight, many paper fortunes that had been built on the stock market were gone. Now, thousands of people were left virtually penniless and without a means to make their own way in the world. It was a daily struggle to feed one person, much less a family. Some families dissolved because of their inability to cope with the situation; others seemed to be strengthened by it.

In spite of severe financial losses, our family wasn't destroyed as many were, but we did go through some pretty tough times. Before the Depression, my parents owned a restaurant and bakery business in San Pedro, California, but had to sell it when competition from the bigger bakeries became too tough. After the loss of our business, the family moved to Santa Barbara where my dad got a job in a bakery. We had to move several times while in Santa Barbara; the rents kept increasing beyond our income.

It was difficult for anyone to find work after the crash in '29; Dad worked at several different jobs. Piano and singing lessons I had started taking when I was five years old stopped.

When I was eight, I started selling newspapers to help out. I had my own corner in Santa Barbara where I could holler the headlines and get a nickel a paper. I was able to keep a penny a paper.

During this time, there was a great deal of public pressure against our country becoming directly involved in the war in Europe. The United States was, however, supplying arms and support to our allies. This brought in more jobs for the people of the United States. Life began to be a bit easier for the people of the U.S. President Roosevelt was establishing many programs to help the people during these troublesome times, one of which was housing for low-income people.

The Depression was finally coming to a close; the people were beginning to recover from their financial losses. Providing the tools of war for the European needs of fighting against the tyranny of freedom aided the U.S. in this recovery. However, rent in Santa Barbara had increased to the point where we had to leave that lovely city. Our father had found a good-paying job with a large bakery in Los Angeles. We moved to Victorville to be closer to his work, where we lived a little over a year. Then Dad was able to buy a partially built house for us and Uncle Rob. It was in a new development in Reseda, a development in the San Fernando Valley located on the outskirts of Los Angeles.

The house was purchased as part of one of the state's low-income housing programs. One of the stipulations was that the buyer was to complete the house. The house had a large room with a kitchen and bath. The back of the house was covered with tar paper, awaiting completion. Dad was good at that sort of thing. I'd admired the improvements he'd made to our house on Bath Street when we lived in Santa Barbara. Now he made bread in the evenings. And when he wasn't working at the bakery, he was busy at our backyard construction site adding two large rooms and an additional bath to the back of this house.

Our mother was working as a live-in nurse's aid for the wealthy Pantages family in Beverly Hills at the "Plantation," which was the name of their luxurious home. I'll never forget how impressed I was with the grandeur of that mansion when my father and I picked my mother up at the Plantation on one of her days off. Until the patriarch of the family died, my mother took care of him. He had started a chain of theaters in Los Angeles, one of which is the Chinese theater where all the stars' footprints are imprinted on the sidewalk out front.

Uncle Rob and I roomed together, as we always did when he stayed with us. A portion of the living room was screened off for us. Uncle Rob was deaf, but he and I had learned to communicate very well. One of my fondest memories of him is when we'd go on our long walks. It was especially fun to do this now that we were out in the country.

We children were doing well in school. We had made lots of friends, and our family loved the house and neighborhood in spite of the fact that it lacked a few amenities. It was on a dirt road out in the country where there weren't any sidewalks. During the rainy days, everything outside the house would turn a sea of muddy water. The streets were constructed so they acted as runoff for the water, turning them into small rivers. It would stay muddy for a long time after a rain as the soil contained a large amount of clay, which prevented the water from soaking into the earth.

Soon after we moved into our new house, we acquired some neighbors. One day, a large truck filled with the belongings of this family pulled up to the house next door. The truck was parked between our houses, and because of the rain the previous day, it got stuck in the mud. My brothers and I had fun watching it slowly sink into the red clay. It sank in all the way up to the axles, hopelessly stuck. I remember Dad going over to see if he could help.

After examining the situation, he built a lever under the rear end of the truck. He pushed a 4x4 down on the lever, raising the rear end high enough for us boys to shovel wood and gravel from Dad's construction site onto the mud in front of the truck's rear wheel. This allowed the truck to have the traction it needed to free itself from its prison of mud. It was able to get onto the road, which—although not paved—was hard packed.

At this time of my life, I would say our neighborhood was a complete mess when it rained. To us young boys, though, the rain brought a lot of fun and excitement.

The family had bright expectations for the future; but on October 17, 1938, our dad was abruptly taken from us. He had injured himself while working to free our neighbor's truck from the mud. He didn't want to complain because he thought he'd just strained a muscle in his abdomen and that it would be better in a day or two. After a few days, though, his health deteriorated quickly.

One morning Dad felt very bad, and he lay down on a cot that was set up in the living room next to the portion screened off for Uncle Rob and me. That's where I found him. He said to me pleasantly, "Hi, Doc, keep up the good work." I think he was trying to reassure me. Mother then helped him to the car and drove him to the Los Angeles County Hospital. That was the last I saw of him. It turned out it wasn't a sprained muscle but a rupture in the wall of the intestine that was causing Dad's distress. I was pretty confused. My dad had always seemed so big and healthy. I later found out he died in the hospital of peritonitis—an inflammation of the intestinal tract, which resulted in the blood poisoning that killed him.

Even though she'd worked as a nurse's aide before Dad's death, without him, Mother seemed helpless. During their married life, Dad had shielded her from the daily economic problems as much as possible. He handled all the finances to the extent that Mom was at a loss as to what to do at his death. Fortunately, Mom and Dad had always been wealthy in fine friends; and with their help, she was able to keep our family intact. This had been the dying request of our father. She received a good deal of friendly advice, some of it wise and some not so wise. She also received, from California's welfare system, a small fund for widows.

The money my older siblings (Bill and Bonnie) made, plus the money I made selling newspapers and magazines, as well as the 25¢ for cutting lawns were deducted from this aid. Eventually, it became such a hassle that Mother decided to give up the assistance.

By 1940, we had accumulated enough money to buy a car and trailer. We prepared to be on the move again.

Several times in the past, Dad's younger sister—Hannah, who lived near Cincinnati, Ohio—had invited us to visit them. We had never accepted the invitation as we had never before had enough money to travel such a long distance. Mother finally was in a position to accept her sister-in-law's invitation.

On the first of June, we set off. In later years, we would become familiar with Route 66 and the other highways we drove over that summer. But on this first trip, it was an exciting adventure. To witness the vistas of our country unfold before our eyes. We were fascinated by the panoramic colors of the Arizona and New Mexico Deserts, the vast expanse of the open country of Oklahoma, and the miles of flat plains of the Panhandle of Texas with its strange plant life. The various species of cacti and scrub brush—such an enormous variety of plant life we'd never before seen. I would have bet that Uncle Rob would know the name of each, but Uncle Rob was left behind in Los Angeles. We stopped often at the Indian trading posts along the way. As I scrutinized the merchandise these posts offered the hot and weary traveler, I could hardly believe how many different colorful and desirable objects could exist in one place. Little did I know then how very much the pleasure we experienced on this trip would contrast with our experience on the return trip exactly one year later.

Chapter 3

CINCINNATI

LIFE ON THE FARM AND IN THE CITY

The pleasurable journey ended soon after our arrival in Cincinnati. We had a nice visit with my Aunt Hannah and Uncle John on their farm, which was about twenty miles north of the city. My Aunt Hannah, Dad's youngest sibling, was very happy to see us. When we arrived, they had just finished harvesting their crop of corn, and my quiet, hardworking Uncle John was busy gathering the mowed corn and putting it onto a large wagon pulled by horses. From there, he took the corn to the barn and separated the ears. He made a pile of the stalks and husks to feed later to his cows. He then plowed the field as the first step in preparation for the next spring's planting.

After all that driving in a hot car, we children were soon busy having a wonderful time exploring the farm. They had a couple of cows to provide the family with milk and a barn with firewood, which we helped chop for heating and cooking.

My brother Bill was the oldest of us children, and he became quite independent after Dad died. He worked at several jobs, mostly at gas stations, to help out. Mother had also become quite independent in the short two years since she had suddenly found herself alone. She had accepted and adjusted to her new position in life. She accepted the fact that she would never be rich but had determined that she also would never be dependent. She left us at the farm to live in Cincinnati where she had found a job in a doctor's office.

The "visit" with Aunt Hannah went well until Mother got that job. We children were to continue to stay at the farm while my mother got settled and could arrange for us to come to Cincinnati too. I suspect this had not been part of Aunt Hannah's plan. I don't think she was expecting more than a short and pleasant visit. Looking back on it, I can understand that, after a while, a desperate widow with six children in tow might have little appeal to any relative, no matter how benevolent.

During our stay at the farm, the four youngest of us boys became quite close. Our first experience in handling money came during the many hours we spent playing monopoly together. This continued after we all joined Mother in the city. Because my mother was living in the city and because I was the eldest of the four of us, I felt a responsibility to look after my younger brothers—especially Jim, who was the youngest. His eighth birthday would be in March, and I thought something special should be done so he knew someone cared.

On the morning of his birthday, Jack and David went to a nearby park to play. It was a beautiful clear day, so I decided to pack a lunch for Jim and me. We found a clearing among some trees behind the house, and the two of us had a little picnic celebration. I didn't think it was such a big thing, but many years later, I discovered how much that day meant to Jim.

One day, during the time we were still living at the farm and my mother was in Cincinnati, the engine of her car caught fire while she was driving to work. A man rushed over to help her put it out. He was Don Hill, a clerk at a nearby hotel. She had found a friend in this unfamiliar city where she was alone, completely alone for the first time in many years.

Mother finally made arrangements for us to join her in Cincinnati. She found one of the numerous lookalike, two-story flats in downtown Cincinnati. So in June, when school was out, we moved again. By the time of this last move, my brothers and I had missed a lot of schooling most of the past year. Because I had been in Cincinnati for such a short period of time, the school didn't have the necessary transcripts of my past grades. Therefore, they wanted to leave me back and have me repeat a grade. As a "know-it-all" teenager, I felt I knew more than my fellow Cincinnati classmates and just hadn't been tested sufficiently for the school to appreciate the extent of my knowledge. In any case, my only failure in school occurred there.

In addition to having to get used to a new school, I had to get used to a new man in my mother's life. As might be expected, I never did like her friend Don very much, but I learned to tolerate him for my mother's sake. It was my older brother Bill who really didn't get along with him, and after one argument too many, Bill decided to return to California without telling anyone.

Bill just decided what he wanted to do and went ahead and did it without consulting anyone or even letting anyone know what he was up to. I guess he just figured that if you don't ask permission or divulge your plans, no one can say no. We younger boys were still "normal," but our older brother was a teenager now.

Bill had never stopped thinking about all the fun he'd had with his friends in San Pedro, and he made up his mind to recapture those good times. One winter evening, he and a friend who he worked with in the gas station left for California. They decided they'd get there any way they could, but it was California or bust for them. It turned out, they mostly hitchhiked and hitched rides on freight trains.

After my big brother left, I began to notice many annoying things that under ordinary circumstances I might not even have noticed. Maybe, due to the stress of all the changes our family had been experiencing, I was more sensitive than usual right now. It didn't dawn on me that I was undergoing changes. In any case, many things seemed to be getting on my young nerves.

For one thing, I wasn't used to living in the city, and I was becoming increasingly aware of some of the unpleasant aspects of being an urban dweller—the noise for instance. Day and night, the clacking of the trolley cars clattering back and forth in front of our house echoed loudly through the dreary rooms of our flat. During the nights, I tried to muffle the racket somewhat by sleeping with my head under my pillow, but it didn't help much to quiet the never-ending dreadful night noises. I finally got an old army cot we had and set it up in the hallway in the middle of the house so the outer rooms would absorb some of the sound; it helped a little.

Another thing I found unpleasant was the weather. I yearned for the wonderful climate of Southern California and hated the cold dampness of Cincinnati. The past winter had been the first time I'd ever touched snow. At Christmastime, while living in Los Angeles, I'd dreamed of beautiful snowy scenes. The closest I'd come to experiencing snow was looking from a long distance at the white-capped Sierra Mountains. They had seemed so soft and downy. I used to imagine how much fun it would be to experience snow up close. *Now snow only represented discomfort to me.* I hated it. The use of coal for heating during the cold, damp winter left a sooty residue that blackened the snow, the icy sidewalks, and even the trees. In the area where we lived, there were few flowers even in the summer, and I remembered all the beautiful ones growing so profusely in California all year round. I wondered how flowers could ever survive in Cincinnati's unfriendly climate. The clean white beaches of California. So much nicer than gray snow!

One of the worst things I was becoming painfully aware of was the unaccustomed lack of friends in our life. I'd always taken a plentiful supply for granted. Maybe people here were so busy trying to recover from their Depression losses that they didn't have much time for pleasantries. For the first time in my fourteen years of life, I found that friends were hard to come by.

In addition to everything else, I felt left out. Mother continued to work in the doctor's office, and Don worked at the hotel. My big brother was gone, and I was lonely and—I have to admit—more than a little frightened. My mother was so busy trying to make ends meet that I felt she had forgotten about her children. I wasn't used to being the oldest son, and I was having difficulty getting used to having Don take so much of my mother's time and attention. She looked the same and sounded the same, but sometimes I got the eerie feeling that she really wasn't the same person anymore.

I was aware that things were rough, but I needed to know what's going on and not be left out. I knew my mother was troubled, and I would have felt better if she hadn't tried to protect me by keeping her troubles secret. Instead of leaving me out, I wanted her to confide in me and solicit my help. Having a helping role to play would have alleviated my worry. As it was, not knowing what was going on made me feel even more anxious. I was confident that I could be relied on in times of stress more than my mother believed. I felt she perceived me as an incapable, dependent child. I didn't want to be a dependent burden; I wanted to be her helpmate.

I found the days getting bleaker and bleaker, and then one day we got a postcard from Bill. He sounded so happy. He had made it back to California and was now working in a bakery in San Pedro where he was learning the business.

I suppose it was that postcard from Bill that finally made my mother come to the realization that we'd made the wrong decision when we'd come to Cincinnati. In any case, Bill's desire to go back to the "Land of Sunshine" must have been catching because my mother soon decided to go back too. One evening, she told us that we were going to return also to California.

At that time, I didn't completely understand why it was necessary to travel again. We'd moved and been uprooted so many times already. We'd only been in Cincinnati about a year, and it was just for the last three months that we had been living in the city. However, I wouldn't say I really disliked the idea of leaving. I'd never been happy in Cincinnati; and I'd been longing for, and dreaming of, the place I used to call home. None of this was home. Where was the love we used to know? This just didn't seem like a friendly place. I realized then that I had taken that past home of comfort and security, of parental attention and love, of a plenitude of friends, for granted.

The plan was that my mother would leave now for San Pedro with my sixteen-year-old sister Bonnie. The youngest of the family, eight-year-old Jim, would travel with them. She would stay with my brother Bill when she arrived.

Then she would look for a job and a place for us to stay, and when she'd done that, she'd send for us. Don would continue to work in Cincinnati to bring in some money and to take care of my two younger brothers and me (twelve-year-old Jack and ten-year-old David) until my mother got settled and sent for us.

I didn't trust Don as our caretaker but was too young to have a say in the matter. I believed that Don was looking to my mother to be his caretaker. It turned out that I was at least partially right about Don. He would prove to be pretty self-centered. After Mother left, he kept working for a while, but left it up to me to look after Jack and David.

Then Don decided to forget about the plan to wait for Mother to get settled and then send us bus fare to join her. Instead, he decided we would hitchhike to Los Angeles right then and save the fare. Don told me of his plan and left it up to me to tell my brothers. He then proceeded to give most of our things away. We prepared to leave without informing my mother of the change in plans.

Don's decision for the four of us to hitchhike across the country to California was shocking and frightening to me; but at the same time, I was very anxious to return to sunny, friendly California and to be a family again. In any case, I was determined that no matter what happened, I was going to look after my two younger brothers. I knew I wouldn't be able to count on Don for much, but he would come in handy because three children making their way across the country alone would certainly be stopped by the police.

It didn't occur to me to worry about the fact that we boys were so young. I was sure that we would be able to forage for food and shelter and to take care of any need that arose. I was confident that we would make it to Los Angeles, somehow, if we just kept heading west. If we misgauged and went too far, we'd end up at the Pacific Ocean. From there, we wouldn't be too far away to find our brother and mother and all our old friends in San Pedro. I knew I'd be able to find my way there.

Jack was convinced that the new plan was great. The idea of taking to the road seemed like it would be a great adventure. The distance was not far on the road map we had. However, I was concerned that our mother didn't know about our plan, and Aunt Hannah and Uncle Steve knew nothing about it either. In fact, we were pretty much in the dark ourselves about exactly how we were going to make it all the way across this big country with almost no money and even less experience. We hadn't yet formulated a specific strategy other than that we would just take off and head west. We were completely ignorant of the hardships we might encounter. At this time, *hardship* was not in our vocabulary. However, we were soon to lose our innocence.

Chapter 4

ON THE ROAD

The next morning, it was cool and dreary again just as it had been every day that week. It was overcast and cold when Jack awoke. He glanced around the drab bedroom and over to where David normally would be sleeping. He saw no one, heard nothing. A chill surged through his young body.

"Did they already leave without me? What will I do if they're gone?"

He panicked at the thought of being alone, leapt out of bed, and ran to the stairs. Then he heard conversation and people moving about. What a relief! He returned to the bedroom where he quickly dressed. Picking up some personal belongings, he went downstairs and joined the rest of us in the living room.

"What time is it?" Jack asked as he entered the room and sat down by a bundle of blankets. He acted nonchalant, but I could see the look of relief on his face, although I didn't know the reason for it at the time.

"Six," someone answered.

"You'd better grab a bowl of cereal before you get your things together," I told him. "It's going to be a while before we eat again."

"Okay," Jack mumbled as he began preparing his breakfast. Because this meal might have to serve as his lunch and dinner as well, he prepared himself not one, but two bowls of cereal. There was plenty of milk, and we wouldn't be taking any with us because we'd have to limit what we carried.

It was early in June and the weather was fair, so we figured the trip wouldn't be too difficult. It looked easy enough on the map. If we traveled in a generally straight line toward Los Angeles, we shouldn't have any trouble making it to San Pedro.

Little David didn't worry about a thing. He was to learn soon, though, along with Jack and I, that the tiring walks would seem never to end, that hunger would become a way of life, and that there was some danger involved in our adventure.

So now, after looking at the map and deciding which way to head, we each selected a warm blanket and a few clothes. We each had a box, which we tied with ropes that were snug but arranged into the form of a handle to make them easier to carry.

"Don't overdo it," I warned them. "After you've carried them a while, they'll get pretty heavy."

We rolled our blankets with a rope in a way that made it also easy to carry over our shoulders. These blanket rolls and our small boxes were all we owned in the world. Each of us was to care for his own belongings, and we each gathered some items of food, hoping to sustain ourselves with them for a while. David opened a can of pork and beans.

"Anyone want a bean sandwich?" he asked.

"Hey, that's a good idea," Jack answered. Both of them got slices of bread, which they covered with a generous layer of cold beans and wrapped them in napkins.

"Where should we put them?" Dave asked.

Looking around, Jack saw that Don had left the room.

"Quick," Jack said. "In here." They opened Don's suitcase and slipped their sandwiches inside one of the shirts.

"We'll get them tonight when he isn't looking," Jack said.

Then off we set, we boys with our blanket rolls and little boxes and Don with his favorite suitcase. We had planned to hitch car rides to California, walking only when necessary so we could conserve our energy. That had seemed like the simplest way to travel. Since I had no shoes good enough for hiking, our first destination was a small shoe store nearby where I bought a pair of tennis shoes—the cheapest shoes available—for fifty cents. We weren't as careful about getting the correct size as Mother would have been. We were just in a hurry to get something on my feet for the long walk ahead. I would regret this later.

Walking through town from the shoe store to the highway, we felt conspicuous starting off on our daring adventure. However, the people hurrying past us to their jobs didn't seem to notice us at all. When we finally arrived at the Ohio Highway, headed west, we tried our luck at hitchhiking. It seemed like no time at all before a man stopped his dark-green sedan and picked us up. I was surprised at how easy hitching rides appeared to be.

David climbed into the small backseat with his blanket roll, his little box, and Don's suitcase. Don rode up front with the driver. There wasn't enough room for all of us inside the car, so Jack and I climbed into the trunk with our blanket rolls. The lid of the trunk was left open, and although it was somewhat cramped in that small space, because we were small, it wasn't unbearably uncomfortable. The only concern I had was that the trunk's lid would close and we would suffocate. We became more aware of the possibility that this could happen whenever we drove over railroad tracks. Jack and I saw stars the first time this happened, and the lid bounced onto our heads.

"Ouch!" I exclaimed.

"Are you all right?" Jack inquired with concern, rubbing his head.

"Sure," I said. "Just a bump. Good thing I have a hard head. Hold on."

I grabbed the lid and held it firmly against the blanket rolls, preventing it from opening far enough to come crashing down too forcefully and also preventing it from locking closed. I was certain the trunk would close, locking us in.

"The spare tire is loose," Jack yelled over the road noise.

"Don't worry about it," I yelled in response. "Just hang on the best you can. Just keep remembering that we're moving west."

In addition to worrying about being locked in the closed trunk if the lid came down too hard, I was also afraid that if we encountered any policemen, they would disapprove of our riding in the trunk of a car. In the imagination of this fourteen-year-old boy, these fears became greatly magnified, especially after being banged so forcefully on the head. I preferred not to share that concern with Jack.

We traveled quite a long distance, or so it seemed, and during the entire ride, I didn't dare release my grip on the inside handle of the trunk. No matter how hard I tried to relax, I was becoming very tired. I could see the highway pavement flashing by and was nearly mesmerized by the view. All I could do was to wait patiently. The odor of the hot tar, burning rubber, exhaust fumes, and the flicking white lines exhausted me. We traveled on and on, and I thought this ride would never end.

Eventually, the driver reached the place where he was to turn off the highway. He pulled to the side of the road and stopped. When Jack and I climbed out of the trunk most thankfully, the driver mistook my gratefulness for my appreciation for his help.

By the time I climbed out of the trunk of the green car, I was exhausted and felt nauseous and dizzy from the car's exhaust fumes. Still, it was a comfort to realize we had traveled quite a long distance toward our destination. No matter that it was a mere few hundred miles out of a few thousand we had to travel. That was the end of the first of many different rides we were to get from many different people.

As the car drove off, we looked around to see where we were. We found ourselves in open country with a tree-lined river on the north side of the highway and down a slight slope. Like us, the river's murky water was racing toward its ultimate destination and moving in the same direction we were traveling. It brought to my mind some of the stories I'd read of the early frontier days. Indians and trappers used this river as a means of rapid transit, cutting through the foaming water in slender canoes. I thought how much easier and more pleasant it would be to travel this way—the clean cool breeze blowing past as I sat peacefully in my boat. I had no idea of the real hardships this means of travel might present.

Since we didn't have canoes, we continued walking, watching hopefully for westward-traveling cars. It was getting late in the evening, and the rides were simply not available. Those cars that did speed by raced into the setting sun oblivious of us four bedraggled travelers.

As we walked along the side of the highway, we passed by several farms and their neatly cultivated fields. We spied some vegetables growing close to the fences and imagined how nicely some carrots, corn, and turnips would supplement the lunches we were each carrying.

"Food," Jack exclaimed, "and it's almost ready for picking."

"Yes," I said. "You don't think it would be stealing, do you?"

"They usually leave the edges to rot," David remarked.

The rows of vegetables grew right up to the fences, some on this side of the fences. The farmer might not notice if a few of his crops were pilfered. Besides, they were practically growing on the public highway's right-of-way. With this rationalization, we helped ourselves to some fresh produce. We didn't think the farmers would notice the little we harvested of their crops as long as we were careful not to damage their fields.

Soon after that, we came upon an area along the riverbank that was shielded from the highway by heavy brush and trees.

"Come on, you guys," I said. "There aren't any cars coming now. Besides, it's going to get dark soon. Let's see if we can bed down by that river."

We found a narrow trail leading to the river, and we followed it until we came to a shaded area. We explored the area and discovered a level spot where we made a small mound of weeds.

"This is just like a mattress," David said. Jack just grinned and kept adding to the mounds. When we'd finished building our mounds, we spread our blankets on top of them so our beds wouldn't be quite as hard and the dampness not as penetrating as lying on the ground. We were pleased with the fairly comfortable bed we had made for ourselves.

"Pretty good," Jack remarked, "if I do say so myself."

"I'm hungry," David complained.

"Okay," I said, "let's clean up this food and see what we've got."

We carried our vegetables to the water's edge and washed the freshly picked groceries in the rushing water of the river. After starting a small fire among some rocks, we tried to roast the ears of corn. Although we scorched them a bit in some places, in other places they were raw; it was with another feeling of satisfaction and accomplishment that we partook of our first meal on the road.

"I think they need to be cooked some better way," complained Don.

"That shouldn't be difficult," I said in disgust.

"Mine is hardly cooked at all," complained Don again.

"It's a little difficult to cook corn the way you want it without the proper equipment," I said a bit testily. I remembered ways of preparing the corn before putting it in the fire pits to roast. Don seemed not to know about this, and I wasn't in the mood to talk with him.

This meal was to be the most food we would eat for many days to follow. Hunger would be with us for most of the trip to California. We would come to accept the craving sensation of intense hunger and overwhelming fatigue as our normal condition, and I wondered skeptically if Don would survive the trip. He left the campfire and went to the river to get a drink of water.

"Quick," Jack said, "we can get our sandwiches now." Opening Don's suitcase, he and David retrieved their tasty treat. The sandwiches were slightly smashed. Bean juice had soaked the napkins, putting a small stain on Don's shirt. With smiles on their faces, they quickly closed the suitcase and put it back where it had been. Tearing his sandwich into two pieces, Jack offered me a piece, which I gratefully accepted.

"That shirt probably is going to become pretty rank," I remarked. Jack and David both smiled and nodded their heads.

Catching fish from time to time hadn't yet entered our minds. We would become more accustomed to picking up what food we could find and learn to live off the land.

However, although we would be able to survive this way, we were to find out that it wouldn't be as easy as we had imagined.

Living off the land is never easy. It would require a more leisure time than we could afford to go fishing very often or even to spend the time to prepare decent meals from what food we could salvage. Instead, our time was spent tramping ever westward—an exhausting, discouraging experience. The distance between Cincinnati and San Pedro was, of course, far greater that we had imagined in our wildest dreams. At times, I wondered if we would ever reach far-off California. How did those early pioneers stand it?

That first night alongside the fresh-flowing river, I climbed into my blanket roll exhausted, many thoughts rushing through my mind, although I wasn't yet aware of all the difficulties we would encounter later in the trip. The rushing sound of the river gently whispering as it passed by was pleasant and soothing. I fell asleep almost immediately and slept soundly, my brothers sleeping quietly beside me.

The next morning, we woke up to the sound of the river rushing past. The sun beckoned to us to rise and shine. However, I wished I could sleep on in forgetfulness.

The morning seemed to be starting far too early, but we had no choice. We had a long way to go, and we had to be moving on.

Chapter 5

THE SECOND DAY ON THE ROAD

When we groaned and climbed out of our bedrolls, we discovered aches and pains in our muscles from all the unaccustomed activity of the previous day. This discomfort would disappear to be replaced by fatigue. We would become accustomed to a sense of perpetual tiredness.

"You awake?" Jack groaned to no one in particular.

"Nu-hu-u-u," was the sound coming from David.

"Come on," I said as I rolled out of my blanket. "Let's see what we can find to eat."

We ate what was left of our previous day's sparse lunch and then trudged down to the riverbank.

"That wasn't too bad a breakfast," David cheerfully remarked.

"Ya," was all Jack could find to say.

I didn't feel like saying anything and was glad one of us had a happy look on his face.

Finding a comfortable spot along the muddy shore, we mechanically splashed the cold river water onto our faces. Instantly, the sluggish cobwebs in our minds disappeared.

"Wow, brrrr," Jack and David exclaimed together.

"Whoof," I said as I splashed the cold water onto my face again.

It was hard to realize that water could be so cold without being frozen solid. I ran my fingers over my face to see if there were any icicles there.

We would soon become accustomed to this new way of life and wouldn't find it so bad after a while.

Meanwhile, the morning was passing swiftly, and we knew we had to prepare for the day's travel.

"Come on, you guys," I said. "Let's get going."

We returned to our sleeping area and shook the leaves, twigs, and dirt clinging to the bottom of our blankets, rolled them up, and tied them with cord, fashioning a comfortable shoulder harness. Then it was time to leave; we would to try our luck on the road again. The sun was already shining brightly, promising a warm day ahead.

The highway was deserted. We seemed to be the only people left in the whole world. We must have looked pitiful trudging along the graveled roadside. Only the wild birds and insects were around, darting randomly on their own adventures. Not a single car was coming or going. The black tar road stretched its lonesome line far off into the distance. The way things had been going, we were going to get nowhere fast. Only one car passed us this morning, and time was quickly marching on.

"Where the devil are all the cars?" complained Don.

We couldn't see another human being in any direction, let alone a car. Jack had a worried look on his face, which didn't surprise me. I touched him on the shoulder and began walking west. David just trudged along unconcerned, resting his faith in his two older brothers. Don said nothing; his face was expressionless.

After about an hour of bone-weary walking, we stopped and sat down on our boxes to rest. I didn't know exactly where we were. A train yard was located not far from the other side of the highway, over a slight embankment; I watched several men working among the railroad cars.

We would come to many towns and cities of this type on our travels. We would pass hundreds of cities and towns like this as well as the homes of many unseen people who wouldn't realize, nor probably care, that we even existed. And if they did, I felt they wouldn't care.

"What are you looking at?" Jack asked.

"Nothing much," I answered. I wasn't ready to share my fantasy of riding in one of the railroad cars I'd been watching until I'd had a chance to mull the thought over for a while. Then, after thinking it over, I felt I'd given it enough thought and decided to take the risk.

"Let's go check out that railroad yard," I finally said to Jack. "Come on, you guys."

"What good will that do?" Don remarked.

"We're not doing any good here, might as well check it out," I told him.

We all gathered our things and climbed the slight rise between the highway and the railroad tracks. There was know one about; the freight cars sat as if asleep on the dark cold rails. Walking near, I saw a coal or gravel car with an iron ladder up each side.

Chapter 6

IN THE RAILROAD YARD

Scattered helter-skelter about on the tracks were many freight cars of varied descriptions. They stood lonely and barren, as though they had long ago been placed there and then been forgotten. The doors of some of the freight cars were open, and I could see that they were empty except for loose remnants of old packing material. Brown paper and straw lay scattered on the floor of the cars. Some of the paper moved slightly in the day's warm breeze, and the lazy movement seemed as though the paper was beckoning to us.

For a moment, the thought came to my mind that the packing material could be used as a makeshift mattress. My hand unconsciously rubbed my sore bottom. It would sure be nice to sleep on a surface softer than the hard ground of the night before.

Every so often, we noticed that a bellowing steam engine would carefully back into a set of freight cars, latch on with a jarring jolt, and then pull them away—for the most part—in the direction we were traveling.

"Sure would be nice to travel that way," I remarked to Jack, pointing out the men who were moving the freight cars around.

"Yeah," David answered. "They even get paid for it."

"Hmm," was the only response we got from Don.

"It sure would be a faster way to travel than the way we had been traveling the past two days," I continued. "There are so many empty freight cars, and most of them seemed to be moving west too. I wonder if we could get away with it."

"I think it's a great idea," Jack said enthusiastically. He was always one to try anything once.

"Yeah!" David exclaimed again, ready to go along with whatever we chose to do.

My feet convinced me that there would be many far easier miles gained traveling by rail than by foot. These new tennis shoes had surely been a bad idea. I must not have bought a pair as big as I needed, because the ends of my toes were being rubbed raw from all the unaccustomed walking we were doing. At any rate, we certainly were going nowhere fast the way it stood. Only one automobile had sped past us this morning, and time was passing. We had to get moving again.

I had heard that the railroad police had to be pretty tough on tramps because the vagrants that hung around the railroads were usually pretty tough characters themselves. In the aftermath of the Depression, money and jobs were hard to come by. Thousands of men were wandering all over the country. Many of them had lost respect for the rights of others.

Besides, there were obviously extreme hazards involved in hanging around train yards and freight trains with their grinding wheels. These vehicles weren't made with the comfort or safety of people in mind. The bumping of one car against another was so shockingly hard, it could easily throw someone under the screaming, angry wheels. It seemed to me that the primary job of the railroad police was to keep people away from the freight cars in order to prevent them from being injured.

Suddenly there was a bone-shattering crash and nerve-splitting squeals as another small engine hooked onto a freight train.

"Listen to that," I said. "It'd be pretty dangerous getting onto one of those cars."

Jack got a worried look on his face. He was waiting to see what I would say next.

"Don't worry," I assured him. "Let me think about how we can go about this. There's sure to be a way." However, I was really wondering if I was fooling myself and my brothers.

I had heard stories about men who had been horribly injured, some killed, in their attempt to travel on freight cars. Had we boys been alone, I'd have been scared to death. However, having Don with us made me feel a little more confident. After all, he was an adult. We would be able to drop any problems that arose on his shoulders. He was sort of an insurance for us. We needed to have an adult with us, and in this, if in nothing else, he fit the bill.

Jack, who was close to my age, I needed for companionship and as my partner in this venture. Jack and I both needed David because the responsibility of protecting our younger brother from danger kept us from giving way to despair.

We would definitely get to California. Exactly how, I had no longer any idea, now that I began to see how difficult it was going to be. We had to survive the best we could, moment to moment, and put ourselves in the hands of God.

Jack was one ready to try anything once. Of course, David would go along with whatever we chose to do. He was already developing the optimistic attitude that would stay with him. My feet convinced me that accruing the many miles we had yet to go would be far easier gained traveling by rail than by foot, or in the trunk of a car filled with exhaust fumes.

Don was hesitant. He lifted his suitcase a couple of times, thought, set it down again, and finally agreed that we should try the rails.

"Come on!" I yelled. Grabbing our bedrolls, I headed for the railroad tracks.

Watching carefully and seeing no one in view, we ran to a nearby coal car that was standing on a side track facing west. Throwing our gear in, we quickly climbed the rusty ladder and jumped inside. There was coal in the car, but not a full load. The inside of the car was laden with soot, which puffed up in small clouds as we stepped inside. Very soon, we had black dust all over our clothes and bodies.

"Good grief," Jack exclaimed. He brushed at the dirty soot to no avail. The mess clung like a magnet. David just sat there on his blanket, wide eyed, wondering what would happen next. We must have looked pretty comical, all hunched down trying to keep out of sight and yet not sit on the dusty black coal.

"Hush," I said. "We don't want those police or workmen to see us." Jack and David hunched down a little more and didn't utter a word.

Time dragged by. It seemed as though hours had passed while we waited apprehensively. Then all of a sudden, the car jerked roughly forward. It moved for a few minutes, then stopped. A little later, it suddenly jerked roughly again, but this time we took off and were on our way. After we had been traveling a while, we all thought that surely we must be well on our way toward California. We couldn't see the countryside. All we could see were the moving clouds above. They seemed to be smiling down on us.

I felt elated. I had vague memories of train trips I'd been on as a little boy, but this was the first time I'd been in a freight car. After a while, we cautiously peeked out of the coal car to see where we were. The car had stopped moving, and we thought we might be in the next town. Much to our horror, we discovered we had only been moving about in the rail yard. We had never left!

Obviously, we had selected the wrong car. The workers had been shuttling this car about the yard. The coal car we were in was apparently going nowhere at this time. There were so many different freight cars, it would be difficult to find one we could easily get into, and we also had to be sure it would be going in the direction we wanted to travel. Disappointed about the situation in which we found ourselves, we climbed out of the coal car. Should we try boarding another car or just go back to the highway and try to hitch a ride? It was difficult to know what to do.

"The only sure way would be to jump aboard a train headed west while it was moving," I said in despair. Jack and David looked at each other, fright in their eyes. They knew as well as I did that that would be a reckless thing to do, especially since my brothers and I were so short. It was difficult enough to get inside the cars when they were standing still.

"We'd better not, Jack," I said. "It looks too dangerous." I could see the relief spread over their faces.

Suddenly, as I stepped down onto the gravel alongside the tracks, a pair of large hands grasped my shoulder. I was scared to death! I was so frightened I got weak in the knees and thought I was going to faint. I knew we were in for real trouble as I looked up into a scowl and a pair of narrowed eyes. The black stubble on the lower part of his unfriendly face gave him a fierce appearance.

"What the hell do you people think you're doing," he bellowed in a gruff voice, which intimidated me even further. He continued to growl at us, then asked us where we were going.

"I could call the police," he threatened.

"Go ahead," Don answered. "Then you'll have to take care of these brats and get them out of my hair."

The workman thought about this for a moment, and it was obvious he didn't care for the idea. He turned his head and spat an ugly stream of brown liquid under the railcar. "We're just trying to get to California as quickly as we can," I piped up. "That's where our mother is." The yard workman had a good laugh at that.

I was relieved once I realized he wasn't a policeman, and he wasn't going to call one. Relieved, but angered too, at being laughed at.

"It's not funny," I said jerking from his grip.

"Okay, okay, don't get pissed," he retorted. "Going to California. Now that's a good one. There are plenty of men doing it, but not kids." He spat again. "Trains are death traps."

We talked with the man for a while about the movement of full and empty freight cars, and he taught us a few things we needed to know if we were going to travel in this manner.

"Listen, I don't want to see you guys smashed under those iron wheels," the workman said. "If you're bound to do this foolish thing, at least learn something about railcars." His change in manner made us relax.

"It isn't difficult to recognize the kind of car you need. There are tags used to identify which direction they'll be heading," he continued.

He explained how the freight cars were picked up by train engines for transport to their destination, even the empties. Destination tags were attached to the side of the freight cars that would tell us where they were going. Although there seemed to be a lot of shifting around in getting the cars to their proper location, it was actually done very efficiently. To us, the main thing was knowing which cars would be going in the direction we wanted to travel. But also, it was helpful to know that there are different types of freight cars. He explained that some carry loads of pipes, others transport lumber, some haul gravel or coal, while yet others carry oil or other forms of liquid. And then there are the enclosed refrigerated cars. Two-hundred-pound cakes of ice are loaded in special holds to refrigerate the cars' contents. Finally, there are the freight cars that haul cargo. These were the ones we were interested in—empty ones, of course. He explained the reason different types of cars were used for different types of cargo.

The railway workman, turned hobo instructor, told us about the revised idea of riding on top of the cars, as was done years ago. He explained that long ago, hoboes rode on top of the freight cars, or even underneath. Now, with the faster trains, it was too dangerous to do this anymore. In any case, we weren't about to attempt to ride on top of the cars. For one thing, it would be too difficult for us young boys, especially since we were carrying our blanket rolls. In addition, we would be too easy to be spotted by the railroad police if we attempted to ride on top. He had to get back to work, and so he left, cautioning us to be careful.

"I'd hate to see your bloody corpses spread over the rails," he said as he walked away.

I don't know if he thought this might scare us off or not. If this had been his intention, it wasn't going to work. As soon as he disappeared, we began to examine the other freight cars, and it didn't take long for us to find an empty boxcar tagged for St. Louis. Several empty cars were on the same string, and we climbed in one. The gaping entrance was high from the ground, and I had to pull Jack and Dave in with me. Don tossed his suitcase up, and he followed right behind it. Quickly we pulled the heavy doors to a nearly closed position, hiding ourselves from outside view. Jack and David looked at me expectantly. I just shrugged my shoulders. Don leaned on his roll and ignored us.

Finding a spot out of sight, we sat down on our bundles and waited. The car was empty except for some remnants of used packing material lying about. Looking around the huge empty space that was our private car, we wondered with an intense curiosity as well as a good deal of trepidation what was going to happen next.

"Would the workmen lock the freight car doors closed, trapping us inside?" I wondered.

The more I thought about it, the more frightened I became until I remembered that the doors of the empty freight cars heading westward had been open. Seals locked the doors on the cars carrying freight. It didn't make sense to seal the empty cars.

"Well," we thought, "I guess the only worry is that a policeman might discover the illegal freight our car was transporting."

"We just need to keep quiet," I whispered. "Everything will probably be all right." Time dragged by ever so slowly, and then I heard a distant rumble. The thumping noise got louder and louder as it approached us. The long string of trains echoed the strong jarring attempts of the engine to start the train moving forward. A huge jerk, indicating that we were finally about to leave, nearly threw me off my perch.

"Ugh," grunted David as he rolled off his blanket roll. Jack and I grabbed at him but saw he wasn't in danger. All of us were shaken by the sudden bump; even Don lost his cool. It was a pretty scary start.

"Riding in a freight train sure isn't as smooth as riding in a car," I said. "But we'll get used to it."

Jack and David just grinned at each other.

It wasn't long before the train began rolling along the ribbon of iron rails, and we could hear the train's typical clickety-clacking as the enormous iron wheels passed over the rail joints. At long last, we were on our way!

Chapter 7

ON THE RAILS

We had arranged our blanket-roll seats in such a way that we could see through the opening left by the freight car's huge sliding doors, but not expose ourselves to the eyes of any officials that might be on the lookout for such as us. The dry brush, the trees, and the various small and large buildings started to speed by us. The train was overtaking the automobiles that were racing along the nearby highway—the same highway that we would have been hiking along, or hitching rides on, if we hadn't decided to risk jumping onto the train. Telephone poles whipped past us at an ever-increasing rate as the train picked up speed. The speed at which we were going was exhilarating. Surely, this was the way to get quickly to the comfort of our beloved California.

The train's wavering, lonesome whistle sounded as we approached and passed street crossings. Some distance away from our boxcar, I could hear the hissing steam escaping from the struggling engine up front.

The approaching darkness signaled the end of a day of education for us. The night air was cooling quickly, and realizing it would soon be too dark to see, we gathered our belongings and unrolled our blankets, which we spread at the back end of the car.

"This is like a giant bedroom," murmured Jack as we wrapped ourselves snugly in our warm woolen blankets. We congratulated ourselves on discovering such a wonderful means of transportation and being brave enough to risk taking advantage of it. During our sleep in our private railroad car, we would be bounding across the broad countryside on our way to California. The clean wind was blowing through the open door of the boxcar; it wasn't long before the four of us were sleeping soundly.

I don't know how long we slept, but sometime during the night, I woke up. I was feeling extremely uncomfortable. The train lurched back and forth, the floor was hard, and the gentle breeze of the evening before had turned into a harsh, cold wind. We got our sweaters out of our boxes.

"Damn it," Don cursed as he saw us putting on our sweaters. "I didn't bring a sweater. I didn't think it would get this cold in the summer. Why the hell didn't you tell me to bring a sweater?" he complained as he doubled up with his shirts pulled tightly around his neck. "This shirt smells like a sewer," he growled. Jack and Dave looked at each other, grinning, but made no comment.

The sweaters helped quite a bit, but not enough. Under my blanket, I curled myself into a tight ball, trying to keep warm. I soon found it didn't pay to change position, as any movement allowed more cold air to come under the blanket. It was obvious that we had chosen the wrong end of the car for sleeping. The rest of the night was miserable for all of us, and by morning, we were stiff and cold. Now we were beginning to wonder whether this was really such a good way to travel.

I'm not sure what we longed for more—to be warm or to be able to sleep. If we could sleep, we wouldn't feel the cold or other discomforts. We were so tired; it never entered our minds to shut the door. We were mighty glad when, after a seemingly endless night, we finally saw the warming sun rise. Then suddenly, we became aware of a silence that was nearly deafening. The train was no longer moving. Despite my exhaustion, I just had to look outside. I got up, and shading my eyes from the unaccustomed brightness, I looked out into the new day. Small sheds stood along the railroad track where we had been deposited. I jumped out of the freight car to investigate what had happened. As I looked around the yard, I saw that the train had dropped our freight car off on a rail siding. That was okay because we figured we must have come quite a distance. The highway, not far off, seemed to be beckoning and telling me that it could still provide help. I saw cars rolling off into the distance on the striped, black trail. I headed back to the car where I had left the others still sleeping. When I got back, the others, groaning with discomfort, were getting out of their bedrolls too.

"That floor was sure hard," Jack said, reading my mind.

"I nearly froze," David complained.

We gathered our belongings and made up our bedrolls. Next time, we'd have to find a way to make softer beds and to set them up on the opposite side of the car from the one we'd chosen last night so we wouldn't be such fair prey to the night wind.

"We'll figure out a better way next time," I said to David. "I was miserable too."

The sweet warm rays of the sun reached out to us when we climbed out of our boxcar bedroom. The train had dropped our empty freight car off onto a rail siding, leaving us alone. Shading my eyes from the brightness, I looked around. We found ourselves in the countryside, and I could see a town not too far in the distance that didn't seem large enough to be St. Louis. On one of the sheds was a sun-bleached sign that told us that Washington was only a few miles away. Too bad, it didn't mean the state of Washington instead of the town. Then we'd be much closer to our goal. We weren't sure whether we were still in Indiana, although we were sure that we were closer to our goal than we had expected to be by this time. But we still had many miles to go.

The freight car sat on this rail all by itself. Nothing was moving in the area except some black beetles wandering among the gravel between the rails. Through some brush, the highway was a small distance away. Now it was the highway that seemed to be our next means of travel. We decided we would give it another chance. At least, there was some traffic there now. A winding trail had been worn between the rails and the highway, and we set off following it. No one felt like talking. We had learned that it was easier to keep our thoughts to ourselves to conserve our energy.

Luck wasn't with us that day. We weren't picked up any sooner than we'd been the day before, but we just kept walking along, placing our hope in our thumbs. Eventually, we came by a farmhouse. The place looked unkempt: paint peeling from the siding, a broken window with a board nailed across the window frame, and the yard overgrown with weeds. On closer inspection, it became apparent that no one was living on the farm.

"Hey," David yelled. We came over to where he was standing to see what had caught his attention.

"There," David said, pointing.

There was a garden with a large number of weeds choking out the struggling vegetables.

"It doesn't seem to belong to anyone," Jack said.

"You're right," I replied. "No one's living here anymore."

As we approached the bedraggled garden, we helped ourselves to food to fill our hungry stomachs. We gathered some carrots, radishes, and potatoes. Because of a lack of care, their growth had been stunted, but they'd still serve nicely on our trip to partially fill the ever-constant gnawing hollow within us, and they weren't fragile. Some tomatoes were struggling to grow on a fence nearby. We picked a few of the juiciest ones and ate them immediately as they would be difficult to carry with us.

Alongside the house, we came upon a well with a rusty hand pump, and nearby, we found a carton filled to the brim with empty fruit jars. We pumped ourselves some of the most satisfying sweet, fresh water to accompany our vegetarian repast. Although this crude meal was nothing to brag about, it served the purpose of filling our bellies. That's all we were concerned about at the time, and we were grateful to the deserted farm for providing for us. After eating and drinking our fill, we felt refreshed and encouraged. "Look, you guys," I said. "We'd better carry some water with us."

"Yeah," Jack said. "You never know where the next water hole will be."

"Won't the jars break?" asked David

"Put them in your blanket roll," I answered.

Each of us picked out a jar with a good lid. We filled these makeshift canteens with the well water, sealed them tightly. We then inserted them in the middle of our blanket rolls. I felt sure this would protect them from breaking.

We gathered our belongings and started on our way to return to the crushed rock along the side of the highway. With the vegetables in it, my box was taking on weight and seemed to become ever heavier as time dragged on. We just kept walking, walking, and walking while automobiles zoomed past, leaving us in their wake. The feelings of refreshment and optimism we accrued at the old farm soon wore off, leaving us once again with the feeling of nothing but utter fatigue and despair.

We were beginning to think there would be no rides to be had hitchhiking in Indiana, if that was where we were. After walking for what seemed like miles, one of the cars that were rushing toward the west swung suddenly off the road onto the roadside gravel. Here was our ride at last. It was the first car that had stopped for us since that green sedan had picked us up in Ohio.

Ohio. How long ago and far away that now seemed.

Chapter 8

THE HAYRIDE

Utterly worn out and ever so thankful to be picked up at last, we stumbled as quickly as we could into the car—an ancient vehicle that appeared to have been rebuilt at least three times. The rear bumper was missing; it looked as though it might have been ripped off in some fierce struggle. The license plate was secured with wire to the broken rear taillight, and red tape was wrapped around the taillight in place of the normal glass lens. The car had no top, and the rear seat was missing; pieces of straw were strewn all over the place. So we settled down for a hayride in this old jalopy. A young woman was holding the shaking steering wheel, giving us a smiling welcome as we settled ourselves on a roll of canvas in the area where a rear seat would have been.

"Where you headed?" the pretty young driver asked.

"California," answered Don, as he adjusted himself into what should have been the passenger seat.

The woman's eyebrows shot up in disbelief. She looked at Don and then turned and looked back at us.

"Well, you've got a long way to travel," she said.

Grinding the gears as she shifted, she got the vehicle back onto the roadway. The engine gurgled as though it were about to die; every once in a while, there was a loud popping through a perforated muffler. Nevertheless, I was hoping for a long trip. The car was a mess, but the driver was friendly and it was better than suffocating. Better than fearing for one's and one's brothers' lives in a freight car. Better than freezing in a coal car, and surely better than trudging any longer on a rocky surface alongside an infinitely long highway under the glaring sun of midday in midsummer in a pair of ill-fitting tennis shoes with the toes cut out.

The car lacked springs, but that didn't deter from my thankfulness for not having to walk. Unfortunately, our release from the march was short lived. It seemed that no sooner had we climbed into the car and got settled in, that the young woman pulled to a stop at a crossroads. We looked forlornly to the right and down the country road she was going to turn onto. The road that crossed the highway and disappeared into the distance. Our benefactress returned our thank you's with another pretty smile and a nonchalant wave and, I thought, with hardly a second thought about the fate of us four poor highwaymen she was returning to the highway.

I felt depression envelop me as I watched the woman speed off into the distance. Here we were again. One foot in front of the other, trudging on and on and on. Walking was becoming my enemy. I looked down the highway, which continued over the horizon. This country of ours was so large. I'd had no idea of its enormity before this exhausting trip. We were far out in the country again, and there were no cars in sight.

Again, Jack and David had lapsed into silence. I kept my thoughts to myself too. They were mainly on the pain in my feet caused by the rough stones along the edge of the road. I thought about the railroad. There wasn't a sign of rails anywhere. I wondered how far we were from the closest tracks. Train riding would sure beat this way of travel. I was concentrating so hard on these thoughts that it kept my mind from the pain the rocks were inflicting on my poor feet.

We passed various highway signs—some with meaningless numbers, others with warnings of curves, a few telling how many miles there were between us and the next town or city. Wheatland: a curious but fitting name for this area of flat farmland. We still were a bit surprised when we came over a slight rise and saw a country school building. Discovering the school didn't surprise us. It was the distance we had walked that amazed us. At the crossroads where the lady had dropped us off, there was a sign pointing this way that indicated the distance to this school. We could hardly believe that we'd walked more than ten miles. Several cars had passed us during our trek but had gone on their way without seeming to be aware of our existence.

Chapter 9

SAVED BY THE FRIENDLY SCHOOLHOUSE

Just in the nick of time! It was lucky we came across the school when we did. Evening was closing in on us, dark rolling clouds beginning to obscure the sky. I could smell the moisture in the air and knew it would soon begin to rain. It was important that we find shelter as soon as possible. The school was empty and looked as though it had been vacant for many days. Here was the shelter we needed. The school's summer vacation provided us with a place of shelter where we would bother no one and wouldn't be bothered by anyone.

"Do you think it's going to rain?" asked Jack of no one in particular.

"It's getting cold," David remarked.

"Yes, I think it's going to rain," I answered. "We'd better find some kind of cover."

We approached the front of the lonely schoolhouse and tried the door. As would be expected, it was locked. We had no intention of doing any damage to the building, but it looked as though we might be in store for a hard and blowing rainstorm, and we wanted to have a nice dry place to sleep in.

While the rest of us were looking for a window to force, Jack found a door in the side of a nearby garage building. It was unlocked, and he yelled to us. We ran to join him, and we all hurried inside the musky building, and not a moment too soon. Almost immediately, the rain began to come—slightly at first, but soon it was a torrential downpour banging on the tin roof of the old building. What a feeling of relief to know that while the ground outside was rapidly turning into a river of mud, we were inside, cozy and dry. We dropped our boxes and bedrolls and looked around.

"Wow, that was close," Jack said.

"Yeah," David responded. "This is much better than out there. I'm so tired."

The rain brought with it a coolness that was welcome at first, but soon, we all began to feel chilled. Once our eyes had grown accustomed to the half darkness in the room, Jack pointed to a pile of wood stacked against the back wall.

"That must be the school's firewood," Jack said.

"Do you think they'd mind if we borrowed some?" asked David.

"There's no fireplace in here," Jack answered.

"The floor is dirt. Maybe we could start a campfire," I suggested.

We gathered a small amount of the kindling used for starting fires. Apparently, the school had a wood stove for the cold winter days. Luckily, Don had some wood matches in his pocket. Arranging the sticks in a small pile, we built a little fire in the middle of the garage floor. By keeping the fire low and small and using dry wood, there was very little smoke. A slight draft under the front door made our campfire burn clean and warm. We all huddled around the welcome source of heat and ate some of our raw vegetables.

"Should we try cooking this?" David asked as he brushed some dirt from a potato he held.

"Naw," Jack answered. "We don't have any pots or pans."

"Raw food shouldn't hurt you," I remarked. "Animals eat it raw all the time. Look how big some of them get." Don just grumbled.

From an empty tin can we found and had washed, we warmed some of our water.

Drinking the warm water reminded us of a long time ago when our Great-Uncle Rob used to drink "hot water tea." He told me how he had enjoyed it on the frontier and when he had lived in England. Of course, he had a bit of milk and sugar with his, but right now it was a welcome luxury to us without these niceties. It wasn't long after this nightcap that we thankfully climbed into our warm, dry blanket rolls. Soon, we were all sound asleep.

We awoke the following morning to a warm, sunshiny day. We thought we'd better get out of there as soon as possible to avoid getting caught by a caretaker or someone else. We ate every bit of what remained of our food and rolled up the blankets.

"Come on, you guys," I said reluctantly. "We'd better get out of here."

"Can I leave this box here?" asked David. "It gets too heavy after a while."

"Yeah," Jack said. "My cord nearly broke a couple of times."

We agreed that it'd be best to lighten our loads by leaving behind the cardboard boxes we'd been carrying. At the pump in the school yard, we filled our jars with water and continued on our journey.

Setting our steps westward, we followed the ribbon of roadway stretching far ahead. We could still see the school in the distance when a large truck rumbled alongside us, squealing to a stop, hissing and sliding on the gravel shoulder. What a pleasant surprise to get a ride so early. Maybe our luck was changing.

Chapter 10

RIDING THE MANURE TRUCK

"Hot dog!" Jack exclaimed.

We ran to the truck. Don got in the front seat with the driver, and we boys climbed over the wooden rails into the flat bed of the trailer. At first, it looked as though it was such a wonderfully large vehicle that it might be like riding in a railroad car. However, it didn't take us long to realize how disgusting this ride was going to be. Strewn all over the floorboards of the truck's empty bed was ugly brown straw, crushed and mixed with steer manure.

The mess was everywhere, and we found it difficult to find a place to put down our blanket rolls. We found it even quite an effort just to find a place to sit. Dave sat on his roll, which wasn't a bad idea. Jack and I stood for a while, holding onto small, relatively clean spots on the side rails. We faced toward the wind so the air blew away the intense odor that was all around us. Bits of loose hay and all kinds of trash swirled about us.

"How gross," Jack sneered. I just wrinkled my nose at him and shrugged.

The air was alive with flying bits of rubbish, which could be blinding. Suddenly Dave let out a howl of pain, and I saw him grab at his eyes.

"Let's see," I said in fear, as Jack and I looked anxiously at Dave's face.

"Wow," I said. "I thought for sure it was in your eyes."

We were relieved to see where a particle had struck just below David's eye, near his nose. There was only a small red welt on his cheek, but it must have been a stinging blow, which I knew hurt like fire.

"I thought something bit me," David said. "It really hurt."

Jack and I nodded.

The litter in the truck was flying about in all directions, small tornadoes of loose grass and all sorts of trash. Facing to the rear of the truck gave us the best protection, and that's what we tried to do.

The truck must have had poor springs or been sprung from carrying a heavy load because it bounced roughly, and we had to hold on to the side rails to keep from falling. There weren't many places to grip. Filth was everywhere. It was difficult to keep track of time; we were so busy trying to stay with the ride. Besides, we never really were too concerned about the hour. Leaving at sunrise and stopping just before dark was our daily schedule. We just wanted this part of a miserable trip to be over.

After what seemed an eternity, I felt the truck slowing. Another leg of the journey was coming to a halt. Climbing gingerly down from the smelly truck, we became aware of the aches and cramps in our muscles from this dirty, jolting ride. Jack and David groaned as they climbed down. I felt foolish walking so stiffly. We had some distance to walk before sundown, but we didn't mind because we needed to limber up.

The truck driver had let us off at a crossroads. We were still in open country, the flat plains spreading all around us. The farmers' plowed fields were long overdue for harvesting, with stalks of wheat bending over from the weight of their thick heads of grain. I marveled at how evenly in height the grain had grown. In some areas of the fields, the wind caused the stalks to bend over even further; and this caused odd patterns, as though some enormous foot had passed through, crushing its prints in the fields of grain.

Alongside the road, near the wheat fields, we were extremely grateful to find a small stream. Climbing down the eroded bank, we took a much-needed wash. Jack and David laughed at each other as the refreshing water cleaned their faces.

"Boy, I'm glad that one's over," Jack said.

"Yeah, me too," David agreed wholeheartedly. After that last ride, this refreshing bath was most welcome, and it soothed into the past yet another unpleasant memory.

Chapter 11

PANCAKES

Satisfied and feeling relieved, we reluctantly made our way back up to the road. Luck was still with us because we hadn't been there long when another car stopped for us. Once more, we found ourselves on the way west. Road signs whizzing past told us it wouldn't be long before we arrived in the next town—Vincennes, Indiana, which was about five miles ahead. The name was not familiar to me.

As the hard road rushed by under us, I felt a painful disturbance that made me grab my neck. Don noticed my sudden move and looked me over. He said there was a tick embedded in the back of my neck.

"Darn!" I exclaimed. "Is it big?"

"Big enough," Don answered. "You probably picked it up from that cattle truck." He had a pocketknife, which he began to use on the tick and on my neck. I think his knife bothered me more than the yucky feeling of knowing a tick was embedded in my flesh where I couldn't see it.

When the operation was completed, I saw the large cow tick Don had removed that had dug itself deeply into my flesh. I was lucky it carried no disease, and the end result was a little scratch that didn't take long to heal. I felt much better realizing the undersized hitchhiker on my neck had terminated its trip, and life.

We hadn't been riding for long before our driver gently pulled off the road. In a parking lot, he maneuvered his vehicle between some other cars until he was properly parked.

"Heck," Jack grumbled. "That was a short ride."

I looked up at a round neon sign signifying a café that offered a tempting menu. My eyes were riveted on colored pictures of various dishes pasted to the café's windows with clear tape. I felt I could eat them all and was amazed to realize just how hungry I was.

"Come on," said the driver as he started walking toward the café. "Breakfast is on me. I'm hungry."

Jack and David grinned at each other. None of us needed any urging.

We went through the café's swinging doors and found a booth with large red plastic seats—seats which, at one time, had been colorful but now exhibited evidence of a great deal of wear and tear. Repairs had been attempted with some off-red plastic tape. We made our way to the restroom at the far end of the café to clean up thoroughly. I took full advantage of the moment and scrubbed as hard as I could. When I returned to the booth, I felt (and looked it too, I'm sure) much better than when I first walked into the café.

The driver had ordered for all of us, and my order was waiting for me—steaming hot and golden brown, the largest pancakes I had seen since my dad used to make them for us many years before. I placed my hands in my lap.

"Go ahead and dig in," the driver told me eagerly as though he was looking forward to watching my pleasure.

I wasted no time in obliging him. I spread all the butter allotted me, and while it was rapidly melting, my mouth was watering in anticipation. In my eagerness, I poured a huge amount of syrup on top. It was delicious, and I enjoyed every savory bite.

David's eyes grew big watching me. Soon, the waitress appeared with the rest of the food. Jack and David carefully prepared their savory dishes just as I had prepared mine.

The wonderful breakfast-lunch put a whole new outlook on this day. I was comfortable once again and pleased with the world. I didn't think of what lay ahead or what we had been through. It was surprising how quickly a little food will affect one's attitude.

Unfortunately, our happiness was short-lived, for the driver said he was turning off here and he left us at the café. Gathering our meager belongings from his car, we thanked him from the bottom of our hearts and sadly walked on.

An old flatbed truck was parked near the roadway some distance from all other cars. Several beehives were tied down on the bed of the truck. Bees were flying all around the truck, most staying among the hives. I thought of the possible stings a person could get and was glad I wasn't the truck's driver. At that moment, the driver walked out of the café.

Looking at us, he hollered, "Want a ride?"

He laughed at his own joke, stepped into the truck's cab without waiting for an answer, and drove off with a hazy cloud buzzing behind.

Chapter 12

THE SHOE SALESMAN

However, it seemed that luck was still on our side.

"I'm going quite a way. Could use a little company, if you'd like a ride," a driver hailed us as we walked toward the road.

"We sure would," we said, delighted to hear that we were not only getting a ride but a long one. As I climbed into the large shiny black car, I felt a bit out of place. I had become accustomed to riding in unkempt and dirty cars. Now we were getting into a comfortable automobile; I could just smell how clean it was. Around us in the backseat, there were several long shoe boxes.

"Just put those boxes on the floor, out of your way," the driver told us. "I'm a shoe salesman, and those are my samples. I'm going to St. Louis. Where are you all going?" he asked.

"California," we told him.

"Oh yeah?" the driver exclaimed. "That's a long way to travel. I was there once, San Francisco, to a convention."

"We're headed to Los Angeles," Don answered.

My joy in the realization that we would ride comfortably for some distance made me feel calm and relaxed. I tried to bring to mind a road map to picture where we were at the moment, but I couldn't do it. We sped out onto the pavement, heading west. I saw a sign indicating we were in Indiana on Highway 50. We must be near a city, judging from the growing areas of businesses and houses, and it wasn't long before its identity was revealed. "Vincennes" was displayed on a big sign with a large population number below the town's name. This meant that we had found ourselves a really good ride at last. St. Louis was the Illinois border town on the Mississippi River.

The road map in my head was getting mixed up because I didn't have much reference to depend on and I was getting confused trying to locate us, but no matter. We were still heading west! My belly was full, and I was relaxed and only vaguely aware of the droning and humming engine. Before I knew it, I was sound asleep.

I slept comfortably and awoke to the sound of voices that seemed to be coming from a different world. I soon realized that we were again invited to a meal. As the car neared a city, a sign pointed out that we were approaching Salem, Illinois. We must have driven through Vincennes while I was sleeping. The driver stopped at a small café and told us to stay put, he would get us a hot dog or something, and he and Don went into the café.

We boys waited just long enough for the midday heat to make the air in the car begin to get stuffy. I was relieved to see Don and the shoe salesman come from the café, their hands full of tissue paper–wrapped hot dogs and bottles of icy Coca-Cola. The brown liquid with dew rolling off the bottles made my dry mouth water.

"Boy, am I hungry," David said.

"How could you be?" I said. "You just ate."

"Maybe so," Jack remarked, "but those hot dogs are sure going to taste good."

"Yeah," I said. "I think so too."

The food was passed around to each of us, along with the cold drinks. I held my Coke up and looked at the bottom. A molded St. Louis indicated where the bottle came from. I bit into my hot dog as the car began to roll; yellow mustard streaked with red catsup rolled from my sandwich. After I'd devoured it, I licked the mustard, making sure none of the food was lost. I was going to stock my stomach in case there would be another long period without any. Jack and David were still gleefully devouring their hot dogs. We finished our Cokes and carefully placed the empty bottles on the floor of the car because the driver would get a nickel refund.

Road signs, telephone poles, and many other types of signs flashed by as I thought of what we yet had to face. I was quite surprised to see the St. Louis sign loom up so soon. The country seemed to be shrinking, and I was continually confused by how my perception of the distance we traveled differed from how far we had actually gone. Since we started out this morning, we had traveled across an entire state.

Chapter 13

NABBED BY THE ST. LOUIS POLICE

East St. Louis loomed ahead as our driver pulled to the side of the road and deposited us. We thanked him for his help and watched the black car pull away, leaving us in the slowly settling dust. I had a foreboding and lonely feeling as I watched the car disappear into the distance.

St. Louis is large, a twin city on the border between two states: Illinois and Missouri. We were outside this large city and knew it might be difficult to get a ride all the way through it. The Mississippi River had to be crossed too, over what probably was a very large bridge. Walking across a long bridge would likely attract attention to us, and that was something we were trying to avoid. We didn't want any delays. We wanted to get to California and our family as soon as possible.

As we walked along, I couldn't help thinking of the railroad, but we were on the wrong side of the city to think of traveling by railroad. Any trains around here would be going into a rail yard or in the opposite direction from the one in which we were headed. As I was thinking of all this, a car stopped in front of us. My heart seemed to jump in my throat. It was a police car! I knew for certain we had come to the end of our trip and must surely now be headed for jail.

"Uh, oh," Jack whispered.

David had a slight sign of fear spreading over his face.

"Keep cool," I told them, pretty shaken up even as I said it.

It would be useless to try to run. The car was already upon us. A gruff voice ordered us to "get in" and we didn't hesitate—Don up front with the policeman and we boys huddled in the back. I wasn't sure if I was about to cry in despair or laugh like an idiot; I was so scared. I was concerned with what might happen to my brothers and me. I didn't want us to become separated. No conversation passed between us as the black-and-white car roared on toward the city. I gazed out the window sadly as the sights of the city passed swiftly by. People of all types, and clothed in all manners, were moving about, free to carry on their own business, not realizing we terrified prisoners even existed. Our freedom had just come to an abrupt end.

The police car seemed to drive in several different directions, almost as though the driver was lost. I noticed that the streets seemed to change names abruptly at unusual moments. At one time we were traveling on Winona Street, which suddenly changed to First Street, then almost before I realized it, we were back on Winona Street again. "Weird," I thought, "how easy it would be for a person unfamiliar with the city to become lost in St. Louis."

"The police station must be located on the west side of town," I thought. We seemed to have traveled so far into the city, and always toward the sunset. Suddenly we were rolling across a low concrete bridge, a wide bridge that seemed appropriate for "ol' man river." I was puzzled. The river must be a state boundary. I thought police authority didn't extend outside their own state. Maybe they were going to deliver us to the police on the Missouri side. Maybe some kind of agreement had been established between the authorities for covering such interstate situations.

The conversation in the front seat between Don and the policeman was muffled by the steady hum of the engine. What charges might be brought against us? Maybe none would be necessary since we were so young—except for Don, of course. We might end up in some kind of orphan asylum. That thought was more frightening by far than the prospect of the unknown we had faced so far in our westward journey. Was it a journey we would be permitted to continue? More than anything else, I didn't want to be separated from David and Jack.

As we neared the far end of the bridge, I noticed that I was seeing fewer blending of tall apartment and office buildings and more lower and more comfortable-looking homes. The city was slipping past us with bush-lined sidewalks and fine green lawns taking the place of the hard gray business structures. Then I saw a few businesses and several motels and a City Limits sign.

"Phew," I thought.

The police car pulled suddenly off the road where only the open country faced toward the west. They had taken us across the city to the outskirts on the other side. The policemen gruffly instructed us to hop out and keep going. These were times when they couldn't handle the many vagrants coming through St. Louis. They didn't want to see us again, and I must say, I didn't want to see them again either. It was a huge relief to have been released from their custody. We thanked the officers politely, and the police car made a squealing-fast U-turn and raced back to the city. We were once again alone and wondering what would become of us. What was going to happen next?

Because we were rested, we began walking alongside the hot concrete roadway once again. Cars sped past us and our need for a free ride. We walked past a sign indicating a city name: Jefferson, which lay some 120 miles ahead. I wasn't sure how far across Missouri that might be, but I hoped it was near the western border. The sooner we completed the crossing of each state line, the sooner we would arrive in California. I still hadn't grasped the vast distance across each state, much less across the entire country there was.

"Too bad we couldn't meet a United States policeman to take us all the way to California," David lamented.

Our luck was still running high; as we rounded a turn in the road, we came upon a railroad yard. There were many cars joined together and waiting patiently to perform their hauling tasks.

"Look!" I said.

"Just in time," Jack exclaimed.

"Do you think any of them are going to California?" David asked.

"Probably not all the way, but maybe partway," I answered.

Several boxcars were empty, and since there was no one in sight, we approached the large iron vans and investigated the white tags attached to their sides like veteran hoboes. We soon found one going to Kansas City.

"Is this the one?" David asked.

"Yeah, it looks like it," Jack answered. "See, that says Kansas City."

"Kansas is way out west, isn't it?" David asked hopefully.

"It's in the direction we want to go, anyway," I answered.

That was all we needed. We tossed our gear up onto the dusty floorboards; but before climbing on board ourselves, we ran back and forth between the car and the grass growing alongside the rails. We pulled a large quantity of tall weeds from the loose ground and tossed them into the car, making a good size stack of Johnson grass. As usual, Don wasn't helping. He just ignored us while looking at a brown, scummy pond.

When we were satisfied with our pile of grass, we climbed into the dark empty car. Our next chore was to spread the stack into a comfortable bed. We had learned our lesson only too well the last time we traveled by boxcar; we weren't going to spend this night with nothing between us and the hard slats of the floor, as we had the last time. This time, we made sure our communal bed was located at the forward end of the car. The wind this night might blow through the open door, but at least it wouldn't be directed at us this time.

After spreading our blanket rolls on the weeds, we settled down as best we could and awaited the outcome of the next turn of events. It was quiet about. David wondered where Don was. He said he was going to take a look. Since there appeared to be nothing going on at this time, I didn't oppose his leaving the freight car. I moved to the door to watch him. David started to walk down to the muddy pond where Don was. Suddenly, the freight seemed to be coming alive. I yelled at him; David turned and ran for the freight car. It was just beginning to slowly move. Getting near the open door, David reached out for me. I grabbed his arm, while Jack grabbed my waist. David swung outward and then into the car with us. David had a gleeful look on his face. I wasn't too pleased. As soon as he was safe, I told him not to separate from us again. I wouldn't know what to do if I lost either of them. It looked like the train was leaving.

We weren't disappointed. We had been just in time. A large, now-familiar rumbling echo began to ripple down the length of the train, and the rolling clatter soon made its way to our car, which lurched sharply forward. The rumble continued past as the rest of the cars were jerked roughly into motion, but the heavy shaking didn't bother any of us this time around, even when a mighty thump set our mobile bedroom onto its way to Kansas along the iron rails.

We sat near the door, which we had left slightly ajar, to watch the countryside pass by. The car was empty except for some rubbish left by those who, at some time in the past, had unloaded our bedroom boxcar. I had a feeling of relief and contentment because we were moving swiftly westward and getting ever closer to California. Small towns rushed past. The endless telephone poles clicked themselves off in time to the clicking and clanking of the boxcar's huge wheels on the track.

Swish-swish, click-click.

Swish-swish, click-click.

The monotonous pitch and rhythm nearly put me into a hypnotic trance. Suddenly, a thought jerked me out of my reverie.

"Where's Don?" I asked, looking around.

"I don't think he made it," Jack answered.

"Maybe we got rid of him and his grumbling." Dave coughed.

It was about then that we heard stomping footsteps on top of our boxcar.

"You guys in there?" hollered a voice.

"Yes, we're all here," I answered.

"I'm staying here until the train stops," Don yelled. "I'll join you later."

Jack and I looked at each other in disappointment. It wasn't long before the train came to a screeching halt. Don scrambled down the car's corner ladder, ran to our opening, and jumped in. It was a good thing he had already put his suitcase in the car; he would have certainly lost it otherwise.

"Why the hell didn't you insist I stay, instead of playing fisherman?" Don barked. "There probably wasn't anything in that filthy water hole anyway."

I looked up at the darkening sky and thought how much longer the trip was turning out to be than I was expecting when we left Cincinnati. Just before night fell, the landscape changed. The flatness of Illinois was giving way to the gently rolling hills of Missouri. Then, replacing the familiar fields of grain, trees of a fine round shape began to appear over the hills. I could still see acres of farmland, some with tall corn growing and ready to harvest, but the character of the landscape differed dramatically from one state to the next. The train crossed several rivers that watered the farmland, and I could easily understand why so many of the western travelers of days gone by had stopped and settled in this state. It was beautiful, peaceful, and green.

After a while, I got used to the odor of rotten food, which seemed to permeate the floor of the boxcar. Bone weary, I climbed into my blanket roll thinking of my mother. She had been born in this state, somewhere near the Arkansas border, in a town called Lineus. As I drifted off to sleep, I wondered how close we would pass to her birthplace. Despite the chilliness of the breeze that blew into our car that night, we weary travelers slept well, although I did wake up a couple of times, once when we stopped in the outskirts of some large city. I presumed it to be Jefferson City. The ringing of the bells, found at railroad crossings to warn cars that a train is approaching, had stirred me into consciousness. Through the damp night air I watched the blurry city lights—some from stores and other buildings, some from traffic signals, some from the cars moving busily about. Afterward, I realized that I had fallen asleep again before we left the city.

I slept soundly until I awoke with a start when the train suddenly jerked to a stop in a large rail yard. I couldn't imagine what city we were in. We had passed through so many of them. And, of course, we were going to pass through many more. I felt confused and just couldn't seem to keep them all straight. It wasn't important. The air of this city was slightly cool, but not uncomfortable. We didn't stay here long; soon the train moved again and slowly wound its way along the backyards of dark, silent buildings. We passed a sign that, in wavering lights, spelled out Overland Park, Kansas City. Then there was a hollow sound as the train crossed an iron bridge that traversed the Missouri River, and we came once again to a screeching halt. The heavy iron wheels dragging on the iron rails. This time, dawn had just begun to spread across the eastern sky.

A yawn caused my whole body to shake. The morning's coolness was unusual and uncomfortable; so I returned to my blanket, looked at Jack and David sleeping soundly, and wrapped myself in my blanket once again.

Some time later, I awoke again to the warm rays of the sun beaming through the boxcar's open door, which was only about halfway open. It was already beginning to get stuffy in the confined space. Jack and David were sitting up, discussing where we might be.

Chapter 14

THE HOBO CAMP

The sleep had been restful and did us good. Now, since we were all awake, we decided we might just as well get off the train here as the railroad police would soon be inspecting the cars. Once again, we went through the routine of rolling our blankets and lacing the ropes carefully around them; we then jumped down from the train.

As we walked alongside the tracks with the rising sun at our backs, a loud, rough voice yelled at us, and I knew we might be in for real trouble. It was a yard worker, telling us in no uncertain terms to get away from the trains before we were squashed like grapes in a press. Apparently, he had no idea we had just arrived as passengers of his dangerous machine. However, rather than cause any further problem, we did as we were told and left the railroad yard. We could hear him grumbling, "Stupid kids, what's this world coming to?"

A few automobiles were roaring along a nearby highway, so we walked in that direction. As we neared the highway, we came by a stream with clean water splashing over large rocks. It looked so inviting that we decided to stop and take advantage of this natural bathtub. Several foot trails led down to the water's edge, and we took the nearest one. Flattened cardboard boxes appeared along the banks of the stream, looking as though they had once been someone's bed. Blackened rocks surrounded cold gray ashes, indicating that someone had paused to cook a meal or just to warm a weary body. Evidently, we had stumbled onto some hoboes' out-of-the-way spot, where wandering people had stopped to rest. People hadn't cared what litter they left behind or what ugly scars they made on the banks of this lovely, clean stream.

As we got closer to the water, we realized that the stream was larger than it had appeared from the distance. We were hungry and grimy. The first thing we did was toss our bedrolls on a piece of the convenient cardboard and kneel down to have a good, although cold, wash. And believe me, that really woke us up. Don said he thought there might be some fish in the stream.

A few minutes later, Jack yelled, "Did you see that?"

Then we all saw the silver flash as a large fish broke the surface and snapped at a darting fly.

"I sure did," I answered. "That looked big."

Jack and I looked at each other with the simultaneous thought about how delicious it would be if we could snatch one of those handsome fish. David continued his morning bath.

"How could we catch one?" Jack asked, voicing his thoughts and my own.

"I'm not sure, but maybe if we have some kind of hook and line in our packs."

Rushing back to our bedrolls, we searched eagerly through our worldly treasures to see what kind of hook and line we might be able to come up with. Jack and I each came up with safety pins we'd used to hold our sweaters together where buttons were missing. Along the riverbank, we found long pieces of old fishing line that previous fishermen had tangled and left behind.

"Get some of that line, Dave," I said. "Let's try to sharpen the safety pins," I said to Jack.

Dave gathered as much of the discarded line as he could find while Jack and I sharpened our safety pins on a nearby boulder. Tying the makeshift hook onto the salvaged line, we attached some old food—probably dried fish from a previous fish fry—from one of the blackened fire pits.

"Do you think they'll go for this stuff?" Jack asked.

"I'm not sure, but it's all I see," was my answer.

The bait was so dry and hard, we soaked it for a while. When it was soft to the touch, Jack and I selected a place along the water's edge and tossed our homemade tackle as far out as we could. Our makeshift "hook" and "bait" were heavy enough that we didn't have to worry about weights. Our lines sailed through the still air side by side. They made only a slight splash as our "great cast" hit the water.

The river's current pulled our lines farther into the middle of the stream, and Jack gave a yell as he fell backward while yanking mightily on his line. The line stiffened as he held tightly to his capture, and we all began to yell together, encouraging Jack to quickly pull his catch ashore. As the end of the fishing line neared the shoreline rocks, his fish gave a jerk and the old line snapped, but David wasn't about to let that food get away. The fish flew from the water, smashing among some shallows with Dave diving on top of it.

Dave gave a yelp. Jack hollered to save his fish, and I stumbled over the rocks to help Jack. We all gathered around the battered fish, which Jack proudly held aloft. Soon we were able to snag two more fish, which we set into a smoldering fire. They were cooked to perfection, and we had one satisfying fish breakfast that made us feel a great sense of satisfaction and self-confidence.

The four of us decided to stop and rest at this hobo camp for a while. It was the tempting fish that affected our decision, and they apparently had been tempting for other hoboes besides ourselves, as we saw bits of bedding lying about. We gathered some driftwood along the edge of the stream and added some to our fire. A small breeze was whispering off the water's surface, cooling the air, and the blaze of the burning wood added comfort to the campsite.

Dave found an old apricot tree growing near the area with fruit ripening on the branches. The apricots were small and some were a little green or badly bruised, but they had a delicate taste, and there was plenty to satisfy all of us. Our fish fry and apricot dessert made a very satisfying meal. It would be nice if we did not have an important trip to consider.

Chapter 15

FROG FIGHT

While I sat by the warmth of the campfire, I gazed at the eddies of the river near the shore. Darting over the rocks and the water were large insects, their long slender wings and bodies giving a lie to their ability to fly at all. A weaving of tiny ants crawled over and under the scarred and battered rocks. The ants were linked between the countless pieces of food that had been carelessly thrown aside and their nest at the weathered riverbank.

A gurgle from the quiet eddy attracted my attention. The movement was caused by two large, fat bullfrogs stretched out on the grass at the river's edge.

"Look at the size of those frogs," I commented, pointing them out.

David started to rise. He was going to catch them.

"Don't! Let them be," I said. "Let's see what they do."

The three of us watched the frogs intently. They were facing each other, staring at each other, stretching their bodies toward one another. Their eyes seemed to be ablaze with mutual hate. Slowly, slowly, ever so slowly, they approached each other. As the gap between them closed, I saw the cause of the coming battle. A green, slightly smaller frog sat quietly to one side, watching to see which of the contestants would become her hero. The gladiators had paused near each other and were staring fiercely. There seemed to be some form of angry communication going on.

"What are they doing?" asked David.

"They're going to fight, I think," Jack answered.

"Yes, fight for their girlfriend over there," I said, pointing.

"I don't understand what they could see in that ugly thing," Jack remarked.

"She looks as though she couldn't care less," I said.

Suddenly, with exploding force, each frog leaped into battle. Grasping one another in wrestler-type bear hugs, twisting and pushing, each frog attempted to overcome the other while still clinging tightly. The battle caused both to tumble into the water where, splashing violently, each tried to twist his opponent under the water where it might drown. Both of them bloated their bodies with air, making it impossible to be pushed under, but the struggle continued with much pushing and twisting. The female sat calmly watching from the bank.

Eventually, the two warriors rolled and splashed out of the water onto the shore. Neither one gave demeanor or sound to the fierceness of their little war. As fast as it began, the battle was over. As if by mutual agreement, the warriors released one another and lay panting on the grass. It appeared to have been a draw, and the female disgustedly turned with a burp and disappeared into the nearby brush. As I watched these poor soldiers who had fought valiantly for their sweetheart's hand, only to be spurned, I thought of the many similarities between animals and people.

When the day was half over, we felt we should end our rest and push on. The river might offer more fish to augment our meager diet, but maybe we'd find similar bodies of water equally generous. Streams were bound to be plentiful on the way west, and we couldn't afford the luxury of pausing too long in any one place.

As we were getting ready to leave, a young man approached the hobo camp, and we greeted each other with the courtesy of fellow wanderers.

"Howdy," the stranger greeted us.

"Howdy," we answered in unison.

"Thought I smelled cooking down here," he said, looking our campfire over. "How's the fishing?"

We told him of our success and then gave him our makeshift line and hooks.

"Here, try your luck," I said. "There're some pieces of fish for bait."

He thanked us gratefully and returned the favor by telling us of one of his survival strategies.

"Early in the mornings, when in a town," he said, "you should stop at some small bakery. If you're early enough, you might be able to find the day-old cakes and rolls that are going to be thrown out."

He went on to explain that since the law in some cities requires that bakeries sell only fresh goods, we could get some good food for free. Thanking him, we determined to take advantage of this information at the first opportunity.

Chapter 16

STRANDED BY THE CARPENTER

Tossing our bedrolls over our shoulders, we trudged once again toward the road. I looked back and saw the stranger throw his line into the river. I then turned my face west; the hobo camp was soon out of sight. We were standing by a highway sign, which indicated that about eighty-five miles down the road, we would come to a city named Emporia.

Just then a car stopped for us, and we were again moving toward California. Usually, I felt elated when someone stopped to give us a lift, but I guess that leaving the pleasant hobo camp had made me feel a little depressed. My negative thoughts kept me from looking around the car or at the driver who had just picked us up. I was thinking that we would make it to California or die along the way. Our lives depended on it.

I wondered if my old friends would recognize me, much less be as glad to see me as I was going to be to see them. And I wondered how Mom, my sister Bonnie, and my youngest brother Jim were doing. This kind of thinking brought on a despondency, which I knew would not help me or the situation at all, so I struggled to turn my attention to my surroundings.

The rolling Missouri hills were becoming flatter, and the change in landscape helped me alter my thoughts and concentrate on the sights flicking past the window. Our driver stopped at a gas station in Ottawa, where we hurried into the convenient restroom to wash our faces. The sink was cracked and dirty, the drain corroded, but the water was clean and it was cold enough to shock me out of the doldrums.

We were back in the car by the time the driver was settling his gas bill, and as we drove away from the service station, I saw that we weren't far from Emporia. We had a free map from the gas station, which we quickly spread out to study our route for the shortest way to the West Coast. It seemed best to go across the southern end of the Sierra Mountains. The map indicated several passes across that grand mountain range, but we hoped to be able to use the most direct one to Los Angeles.

Satisfied that we were traveling along the best route at the moment, we folded the map just as we rounded a turn leading into Emporia. The driver dropped us off at a crossroads entering the city, and before we'd walked very far, we were attracted by another railroad yard. There was a lot of activity going on in the yard, so we quickly decided against opting for train travel this time. The chances of getting caught were too great; we decided to head back to the highway.

Just as we made this decision, an old and dirty car slid to a halt behind us, and we gratefully climbed in. The seats were worn and torn in several placcs with wiry horsehair poking threateningly out, but we were happy to have a ride. The man obviously didn't care about the appearance of his car and counted on it only for transportation. We guessed right away that he was a carpenter because the back of the car was strewn with the tools of that trade. Seeing those tools brought back memories of my dad.

The carpenter had removed the backseat to make room for his tools—among them, three saws and an open wooden toolbox. Although the lid of the box had been fitted for his saws, they hadn't been put back there; instead, they had been carelessly thrown to the side. The two hammers were badly dented at the working end, and black tape was wrapped around the fractured handle of one of them. Nails were mixed with trash and dirt on the floor.

Such a contrast from my memories of my dad's neat work habits and careful attention to his tools. He used to say, "Take care of your tools, and they will take care of you." Made good sense to me.

In spite of the clutter, we sat comfortably on our bedrolls where the seat had once been. We sat around a cardboard box partially filled with beer bottles and placed where the driver could readily reach them. He was quite a talker, complaining loudly to Don about the lack of work. He said he was returning from Emporia, where he was supposed to have had a job. The job had been canceled, but no one had bothered to notify him that morning. Now he had wasted his money on this round trip, and this lost day would never be made up. He told us that if he was able to get some work, he wouldn't report the income so he'd be able to keep all of it and make up for what he'd lost today. I wasn't sure what he was referring to, but his growling was beginning to get on my nerves.

The carpenter went on to say that there would be little chance of getting any work this month because there was some kind of hold on building. The only thing he could hope for would be some kind of repair job. Between his complaints, he kept offering us some beer. Don accepted, but we boys refused. The smell of the beer wasn't very appealing, and we didn't think the taste would be any better. The beer brought back my memory of the only time I had ever seen my dad drink anything other than black coffee. He and I had just returned from a deep-sea fishing trip, and it was a hot day. He opened a can of beer then, but that was the only time I saw him drink it.

I was returned to the present as the car entered a small town. The driver slowed neither his car nor his steady stream of complaints. Not seeming to be aware of his passengers, he sped through the streets of the town, pulled into a driveway, and stumbled clumsily out of the car. Waving at us but without saying good-bye, he entered the house.

We were taken completely by surprise. He had left the highway several blocks back, and we found ourselves stranded in a run-down residential neighborhood.

The worn-out-looking houses badly needed paint. From the ancient wood lathes hung large pieces of old color peeling off in ragged shapes. The yards were overgrown with weeds. The brush growing in front of this house where we had so unexpectedly and unceremoniously been unloaded had long been in need of trimming. It grew clear to the edge of the property. We looked around, bewildered, wondering where we were. As we started walking, a city bus rumbled to a stop at the corner, so we climbed on board.

We felt a little self-conscious about our appearance and that of our gear, but there weren't many people on the bus. We dropped our nickel in the receptacle and took a seat. The driver absently flicked a lever and cranked a handle, which performed a count while the machine devoured our coins. Happily, the bus took us completely through the small town and, at the city limit, turned into a large, flat, and open field.

"End of the line," the driver announced. He shut off the engine and opened the folding door and stepped out. We followed him nonchalantly and without comment, just as though we knew what we were going to do next.

We found ourselves on the highway once again, but we couldn't tell which highway it was or where it was going. Having no other choice, we just started walking, hoping to come across a road sign that would set us straight again. A sudden shiver reminded me that it was getting late in the day. At this point, we were completely disoriented and discouraged. After all we'd been through, California still seemed so far away.

"Boy, that guy sure was something," Jack commented.

"Who?" asked David.

"That carpenter who gave us that last ride," Jack answered.

"Yes," I said. "He didn't exactly seem to have half his senses. I think he was drunk."

"I thought he was mad at us," David said.

As we prepared to try to hitch another ride, I heard a familiar grinding of metal accompanied by a long drawn-out squeal. Our unknown highway had been built along another rail route. Instead of hoping for a car hitch at this late hour, we decided to investigate the railroad again.

Chapter 17

THE REFRIGERATOR CAR

Up a slight grade, off the opposite side of the road, we saw a long line of refrigerator freight cars sitting on a rail spur. These large boxcars, with means of storing huge blocks of ice to keep produce fresh, were just sitting quietly while the engine, far ahead clanging and puffing steam, was getting ready for the coming journey.

After taking a glance, I said, "Come on, let's see what's there."

We all clambered up the steep bank to the rails. Walking along the side of the freight cars, we watched for rail men who might chase us away.

The refrigerator cars had been secured. Some were empty but looked fearsome with their strong bars binding the doors shut. The more we thought about it, the more frightening became the thought of attempting to board one of these food carriers. It appeared that the doors could all too easily close, preventing escape. The idea of being locked behind one of those formidable sliding doors caused us to discard any consideration of using the ice cars for a night's sleep and a ride.

"I don't like the idea of getting inside this icebox," I said.

"That seems to be all there are on this train," Jack commented.

We knew we had better make up our minds right away. Our desire to get to California as soon as possible was what settled the matter.

"Are we going to sleep on the ground tonight?" asked David.

"No," I said. "We're losing too much time that way. We need to keep going."

"What then?" Jack asked, looking up and down the freight line.

"We'll just have to find a way to prevent the door from closing," I answered. I thought that if we were careful, we might be able to do it safely.

We chose one empty car scheduled to head in our direction and climbed on board, but as we did, we set a large boulder securely in the slide track of the door to prevent its closing entirely. We then stuffed a large amount of Johnson grass at the front of the car for our bed.

Before we had settled into our compartment, a noise indicated that someone else was climbing into the car. I was relieved to see just another rail bum looking for a free ride. Moments later, two others also climbed in: a couple. A little older and more wary, they moved to one end of the car and sat there talking quietly. The first young man who climbed into the car after us had noticed some fruit that had dropped between the slats that covered the freight car's floor. These allowed air to circulate around the food stored in this type of railcar. Apparently, a box or sack had broken open, and some fruit had dropped through. Lemons and potatoes were lying about under the slats that were too close together for a grown man's hand to reach through.

The young man was really struggling to get at the fruit, and seeing his lack of success reminded me how hungry we were too. I volunteered to get the fruit and easily reached through with my smaller hands, working several pieces through the slats. I gave the lemons to the young man. He told us his name was Tony and thanked us for the help. He then squeezed the lemons into a jar, and we mixed in some of the water we had. We passed around some of the crackers we had saved from the café. Then we wiped the potatoes as clean as possible. Eating raw potatoes wasn't new to us; the starchiness was hardly noticed as our bellies gratefully accepted the cold meal. The lemon juice made our lips tingle, and our bodies shook uncontrollably; but we gulped down the tangy-tasting drink, knowing we needed both the liquid and the vitamins.

"That's not too bad," I said.

"Needs sugar," Jack commented.

David just looked at us both while he finished his bitter meal.

After our small supper, we settled into our blanket rolls; we were soon covered in darkness. Night shadows obscured the buildings, trees, and other objects as our train sped past. The rumbling of the refrigerator car rolling over the rails—clicking rhythmically, hypnotically—drifted into the distance as I fell asleep.

The lurching of the train as it came to a stop the next morning acted as an alarm clock for me. By this time, I had grown used to the sudden jerks and the noise of the freight trains' squeals and the many metallic sounds that surrounded us. I hardly noticed the constant bumping together of the cars as they swayed back and forth fiercely. But when the train stopped, the quietness closed about me like a large envelope, and all the nerves in my body quickly signaled the change in motion. I was never able to sleep through such sudden changes into silence and stillness.

Looking about the empty refrigerator car, I discovered we were alone once again. Our fellow passengers must have disembarked while we were still sleeping. Outside the car, there was no sound or movement. I shook everyone awake, and we quickly gathered our belongings and climbed down from the car. It was dark outside, but in the east, we could see the false dawn trying to struggle into life. The new light was trying to push back the star-spangled darkness of the sky. It was a battle we saw repeated many mornings during this trip, a battle the dawn and darkness both wished to win. The daylight, as usual, was successful. This morning the victory was a magnificent splendor, followed by a rush of the fresh day's air. I failed to appreciate all this at this time.

Leaving the silver strands of the railroad tracks, we hiked down a dry and dusty road into a sleepy town. A few people were milling about, beginning their morning routine. A small bakery glowed with light, and the delicious odors from its enticing products poured onto the street.

Chapter 18

SPOILS OF THE BAKERY

Remembering the story told to us by our hobo friend a few days back, we entered the back entrance to the bakery. Two men were working with flour sacks draped across their waists. A fine mist of flour covered the floor, and the arms of the men were speckled with bits of dough. We asked the bakers for any day-old rolls they might have and offered to carry out their trash and sweep the floors in trade. They were pretty surprised when they heard the offer. We thought bakers must be a kindhearted lot because they found plenty of trash for us to dispose of. It appeared to me that they went out of their way, for it was obvious they had already removed most of the daily trash themselves, but they found some more for us to get rid of.

At the back of the storeroom, several pans of cakes, cookies, rolls, and bread were set aside. One of the men got a large brown paper bag and filled it with some of each, except for the cakes. He handed each of us a small cake to eat and some hot coffee to drink using four of the several old cups hanging from nails over a stained deep sink. I felt like Hansel of the children's story I had read long ago. It was the best food we had eaten in a long time.

Jack said, "I remember when Dad would bring home day-old cookies and lots of bread from the bakery."

"Yes," I said. Some of them had been so old, we had to pick out small spots of mold. In those days, we had bread pudding often. David said he remembered that too, but didn't remember Dad bringing home any cakes like these. Dad had usually made the cakes and pies at home.

Leaving the bakery, we must have been a sight: walking down the quiet street with our bags of food and blanket rolls over our backs, stuffing ourselves with cake and hot coffee. I don't remember what we did with the coffee cups. The baker had told us to keep them.

Chapter 19

INSIDE THE SEWER PIPES

After finishing our delicious breakfast from the bakery, we headed back to the freight yard where we sat contemplating our situation. The plan was to travel in a west-southwest direction so as to arrive at Los Angeles via the most direct route; we knew we still had the Rocky Mountains to get across. This was shown to us from the road map we still had. The Rockies, the Continental Divide of our nation, were supposed to be a series of deep canyons and high, steep mountains. I tried not to think about that part of the trip—yet.

We still had a long distance to travel. We were in Kansas. Just where in Kansas, I wasn't certain; but I knew we had Colorado, Utah, and Nevada still between us and California. And plenty of unknown dangers and hazards were likely to confront us along the way. We had become considerably better-seasoned travelers of the road than the innocents who had begun this trip just a few weeks before.

When we returned to the rail yard, we found a train in the process of being assembled for a trip. We looked the boxcars over for any possible empties. There were none so far as we could see, but there were several flat cars with enormous pipes tied securely onto them. The pipes were large rusty tubes used for sewer construction before the days of concrete sewer pipes, and there was plenty of space in this cargo. We climbed the ladder to a nearby car and settled ourselves inside one of the pipes.

"It's plenty warm outside," Jack said. "These pipes will give us shade."

"Yes, it will," I said absently.

David was trying to place his roll in a secure place within the rounded tube. We expected the wind to blow through the pipes pretty strongly. It wasn't long before we were lunged forward, and we were on our way. We found this rumbling leg of the rail trip to be far less comfortable than the previous rides on the inside of a boxcar.

The wind blowing through the pipes forced us to wrap ourselves tightly in our blankets and huddle together to stay warm; but still, we were shaking with cold. We had a good view of the passing countryside, and we had protection against the elements in the unlikely case of rain, but there was no protection from the wind. It howled terribly and ceaselessly all around us.

Soot from the engine funnel far ahead of us blew back, adding to our discomfort. The black and sticky particles settled everywhere, even inside our blankets. That evening when the train pulled into an obscure town, we were black with soot. Looking like coal miners, we left the pipes and quickly decided that the limited protection afforded by that type of freight car was not worth the dirt and discomfort. We walked up and down the line of cars hoping to find better accommodations for the night. We definitely didn't like the idea of riding those pipes all night long. The cold and soot would be unbearable.

Looking worried, Jack said, "Those pipes were no good."

"I kept my eyes closed," David remarked. "I was afraid that the soot would get in my eyes."

"Looks like it's the ice cars again," I said.

"That's okay with me," Jack answered. "That last one wasn't bad."

"Maybe we'll find some more lemons," David added.

Chapter 20

RIDING IN THE ICE COMPARTMENT

We looked and looked for a suitable car. However, this train was far more closed than the others we had encountered. All of the cars were sealed, and most of them were refrigerator cars. Some of the cars were tagged as being empty but were nevertheless sealed closed.

"It doesn't look like any are open," Jack noted solemnly.

"Maybe the ice compartments are empty," I said. "Let's check."

We climbed up a side ladder to the top of one of the cars to check the ice compartment where two-hundred-pound cakes of ice were placed. These provided the cold for the perishable goods. We looked for the ice hatches to locate a space suitable for a bedroom. The opening was on the top far end of the car and designed to receive the huge cakes of ice. To hold those enormous cakes of ice, the space had to be reasonably large throughout, possibly as big as a third of the room in the car itself. We found that the ice compartment did allow a cozy place big enough for all of us. Since the train was preparing to leave, we didn't have much time to ponder the situation.

We settled for the one we were staring into. It was quite deep, stretching from the top to the bottom of the car. There were two trapdoors at the top, with wooden ladders leading to the lower part of the compartment. The space at the bottom had ample enough room to allow two of us to lie in our blanket rolls, side by side, while the other two could lie in the opposite direction. So long as we lay with our heads almost touching the sides of the compartment, we just made it in a tight fit.

We left one of the hatches open for air. I wasn't sure how airtight the space really was, but it stood to reason that the hatch had been designed to keep evaporation to a minimum. If that was the case and the hatch closed during the night, we might suffocate.

Jack started in with his perpetual worrying again.

"What if they decide to put ice in here?" he asked.

"I don't think they'll do that tonight," I answered.

I must not have sounded convincing because Jack continued to give voice to his concern. Our fears fed on one another until, finally, Jack and I decided to set a watch.

"I'll take the first watch," I said. "You go on to sleep, and I'll call you when it's your turn."

"Okay," Jack said. "That sounds like a good idea."

I climbed to the top of the wooden ladder and stood there, watching the hatch and the stars in the dark black sky. It seemed fairly simple at first. I wasn't sleepy, and I felt so much more secure knowing that ice wouldn't be put into the hatch while we were all sleeping, oblivious to what was happening. Time passed slowly, though, and my only diversion was the night sky that was passing by above me. Once, I tried sticking my head out to see if it might be more comfortable on top. Soot and insects struck my face with stinging blows, and I quickly retreated. I was lucky I didn't get something in my eye.

Eventually, I began to get tired and found my eyelids drooping. It became a continual fight to keep sleep at bay. I began to feel that time was standing still or running over and over again like a broken record. The only company I had was the noise of the rushing wind passing by the opening, the rhythmic clicking of the iron wheels passing over the rail joints, and the jerks of the train shaking me every once in a while. I felt really lonesome.

To pass the time, I tried remembering the multiplication tables I had learned in school. I worked out problems in my head then found my thoughts wandering to my friends of the past. They wouldn't believe me if I told them what I was doing now.

Every so often, I thought about waking Jack to take his turn at watch but would put it off. His turn would come soon enough, and then he would have to pass his time by keeping his thoughts on something. "He deserves this rest," I thought. I really had no idea just how much time had passed since I had started my watch, but I was certain it was well past midnight. Finally, after I had almost slipped from the ladder in my drowsiness, I climbed down and shook Jack awake. He took the watch and told me in the morning that he just knew they would start to fill the space with ice during the night.

We spent a pretty miserable night with Jack worrying most of the time, but it was another valuable experience to log away in our minds. Never would we ride one of this type of freight car again. It would have been better to sleep in the brush at the side of the tracks and try for a ride the next day. We were becoming well acquainted with our traveling companion: misery.

Chapter 21

STRIKING GOLD

I can't begin to tell you how relieved we were to leave that ice compartment. It seemed that anything would be better than that; and the next day was better—but not by much! After leaving our refrigerator bedroom, we motley hoboes continued to look for free rides.

After our frightening night in the refrigerator car, we found a freight train's boxcar; climbing on board it put more miles behind us. However, this train had then turned our boxcar off onto a siding. It then dropped two or three cars before the train continued on. As luck would have it, our car was one of those left behind. We had been frustrated by similar experiences in the past when riding the rails. The train would turn freight cars off onto a siding where it might stay for hours. The railroad often put empty cars off on the side rails to allow passage to fully loaded trains on the main rail. At times we saw passenger trains pass, their cargo of warm and well-fed people gazing at us through their double-paned Pullman windows. They were always attractively dressed in their traveling finery, looking comfortable and at ease and making me extremely conscious of our rags and weariness. This was another one of those days.

After waiting a while and feeling the heat of the sun bore into us, we decided that we might as well move on. Jumping from the hot steaming car, we set off along the ever-endless tracks. After a while, we left the rail yard and hoofed it over to the highway. This too led to frustration. We found ourselves stranded far out in the barren countryside more than once. The drivers who eventually picked us up after we had walked long distances would invariably have to turn from the highway far short of where we expected them to be going, and we would have to try hitching a ride all over again.

It was beautiful country through which we now walked, and if our moods had been better, we might have enjoyed the day. Just off the right-of-way, a rocky slope led down to a foaming river, which cut its way through the surrounding hills. Trees of all shapes and sizes spread across the broken landscape, and the greenery looked cool and comforting. The river seemed in a great hurry—smashing into large rocks, sending a spray of water high into the air, and then falling back down in a curtain that splattered into the little ponds gouged out of the riverbank. The calm, clear water was blue and deep—so clear, we could see far down into little ponds created by the twist and turn of the river's path. Huge fish swam about, seemingly in slow motion. On another day I surely would have savored the sight, but on that day, we were discouraged and didn't avail ourselves of the opportunity to appreciate the wonder and beauty nature offered us. We just trudged sullenly right on by this lovely river.

After walking for what seemed an eternity, we came upon the entrance to some type of mine. The land was lonely, with only the rusty tracks winding through the hills; below the tracks, the crashing river was searching for its home.

Our curiosity got the better of us. We stood at the opening to the mine. This was the diversion we needed from our monotonous trek, so we gave in to a boyish desire for some fun.

"What do you think is in there?" Jack asked.

"Maybe gold," David answered.

"Maybe," I said. "I think this is gold country."

"Maybe we can find some gold and get rich," David said enthusiastically.

"I doubt it," I said.

"Where do you think the people are?" asked Jack.

"I think this is a weekend," I answered.

Our imaginations quickly went into play when David pointed out a coal car sitting alongside the main track.

"What's that?" David asked.

"A coal car," Jack answered.

"It's full of rocks, not coal," David said.

"I think that's ore," I said.

"Gold ore?" David asked.

"Maybe," I answered.

The cars were loaded with crushed and broken rocks, which apparently had been dug from the mine. Most of the rock was whitish or discolored quartz, which we soon found was streaked with a yellow color. Picking out some pieces to examine more closely, we found that the rocks were streaked with faint bits of golden flakes. When we pressed these flakes with our fingernails, they seemed malleable like soft gold. The ore was not very good, but there was a trace of gold nonetheless. We searched the area for something we could dig out the softer gold with. A lot of rusty old metal was lying about, but there was nothing that we could use to dig out the gold.

Having satisfied our curiosity about this unusual area, the three of us boys loaded our pockets and bedrolls with the best ore we could find. Jack considered himself rich already, and I must admit, I felt a definite lift to my spirits also. Don knew nothing of this because, while we boys had been making our fortunes, he had been more interested in looking for food. He'd had no success, although he had found a source of fresh water, and of course, there was plenty of water available from the river below as well.

Reluctantly we left this intriguing and rejuvenating place, setting a pace along the westward tracks again. Jack and I were already devising schemes of what we might do with our pockets full of riches, though before many miles had passed we began to reconsider. The weight of the ragged rocks became more and more apparent, and our steps started to drag under it. We decided perhaps there wasn't much richness in the gold we had, after all. In any case, even if we lightened our load a little, we wouldn't feel we had thrown away all chances of hitting it rich. Before we'd left the mine area, Jack had secretly stashed some ore in Don's precious suitcase; and after a while, he too began to feel the extra weight. He mumbled that he certainly seemed to be getting tired earlier this day.

David took some of the ore from his pocket and began tossing the rocks into the river below. Jack and I wondered what might happen if a prospector came upon it. We laughed at the idea of what he might think, and we joined David, tossing our ore into the river to "salt the find" for our imaginary prospector. This, of course, lightened our load and made the walking easier—so much so that, after a while, even Don noticed. He was sweating from carrying his unexpectedly heavy load and sat down to rest. Suspiciously he opened his bag. It was not a good time to try to talk to him as he cursed angrily and threw his extra load into the bushes. None of us was willing to admit just who was responsible for his extra burden. Frustrated, he gave up trying to place the blame, venting his anger in curses on the whole world in general and on anyone within hearing distance in particular.

Even Don's anger disappeared shortly, however, as we soon came upon a small cove cut from the side of the hill by the river. A small green clearing surrounded the cove, inviting our closer inspection. We found that the swirling river current had created a fine sandy beach at the water's edge. No great architect could have formed a more beautiful spot. The coolness of the pond beckoned us, and we found we could not deny it as we had denied the temptation of nature a short time ago. It took no deliberation at all to decide that this was going to be our camp for the night.

We broke a trail through the brush down to the cove and were delighted with what we found. The clean white sand had been ground by the action of the river over hundreds of years. The stillness of the pond, fed and drained by one small inlet from the mighty river, seemed to have been designed especially for us. We paused long enough to select a spot for a decent bed, where we could spread our bedrolls on a mattress of weeds and sleep in comfort that night. Then we headed lickety-split for the water. David was the first one in, and the rest of us were hard on his heels.

Chapter 22

FISHING SPEARS

Jack hadn't been wet long before he let out a yelp and pointed to two large trout sharing the pond with us. They appeared to have stranded themselves, or at least thought themselves stranded, although it looked to us as though they could easily have escaped back to the river through the small access stream.

"Look at the size of those speckled fish," Jack exclaimed.

"Can we catch them?" asked David.

"We can always try," I answered.

The anticipation of another fish meal made our faces brighten. We all looked about for some tool to catch the fish before they escaped.

In great excitement, Jack broke a slender limb from a nearby bush, which Don sharpened with his pocketknife. Dave set up a guard at the inlet, and I watched at another small stream that also fed into the river. We weren't about to let this surprise supper get away. Don tried unsuccessfully to snag the fish with his homemade spear, but each time he approached, the fish darted to the opposite side of the pond. As usual, Don quickly lost patience; cursing in anger, he tossed the spear aside.

Jack took the makeshift gaff. Feeling its weight carefully, he began to stalk his prey slowly. He didn't seem to be having an easy time of it. Jack discovered that the water distorted the target, and when he jabbed directly at the fish, they were slightly off his line of sight. He found he had to be not only quick but skillful as well, despite the fact that in the movie films wild bears seemed to make it look so easy. The bears had lifelong learning experiences to aid them.

Jack quickly developed his art, and when he finally ran his spear through one of the fat fish, he hollered loudly in delight. I jumped in to grab his capture by the gills, bringing it to the surface and then quickly tossing it well up onto the beach. Don retrieved the trout and built a small fire among some rocks on the sand. Jack and I returned to our stations at the pond, and Jack—with his newly found skill—soon had the other trout caught and flung ashore. Both fish were easily a foot long and very fat. David clapped his hands, jumping up and down with glee.

Don cleaned the fish, removed their heads and tails, and inserted a stout green stick through them and held them in front of the campfire. The smell of those trout roasting over the campfire was heaven to my nostrils. The fragrance was so delicate, it brought the anticipatory juices flowing in my mouth. No need for seasoning or cornmeal here. That crisply cooked white meat fairly melted in my mouth. Some future day, those extras might be important for a fish dinner; but for now, we were having a banquet that required nothing more than the fresh trout, some rolls remaining from our stop at the bakery, and the pure sweet water from the river. Whatever hardships we had endured up to now were completely forgotten as we picked the fish bones clean.

That evening, we rolled into our blankets, quite thankful that we had spent our gold for such a delicious meal. The beauty of the river had finally come through to us, and we fell asleep with red and gold color splashing the western skies and the gentle sound of the river filling our ears. My mind and thoughts were finally at ease.

Chapter 23

DENVER:

THE SALVATION ARMY TO THE RESCUE

The bright sun of the next morning woke us up. We awoke feeling rested, comfortable, but once again, hungry. We ate the remainder of our bakery gifts and washed it all down with warmed river water. It was a meager breakfast, but it would have to do.

We performed the familiar task of getting our gear together, taking a little extra effort to make certain we'd shaken all the sand from our blankets. I noticed that Don took care to check his suitcase for undesired extras. Taking one last look around this very special campsite, we set out on the next leg of our wearisome journey.

By following the wide wooden ties that held the rails to the ground, we eventually came to a highway; and since the railroad appeared to be inactive in this area, we elected to take to the road for our alternate hope of transportation. Again, the countryside seemed to be changing, this time from plains to rugged hills. Generally it was still plains, with lots of grassy areas and a variety of broad-leaf trees, mostly oak. The ground was becoming more and more rocky, with large abutments of boulders pushing toward the highway out of the rough cliffs. Shale and sandstone were more exposed at the sides of the road where the weather had chewed into them, creating weird patterns. In the distance, somewhat toward the west and south, I could see enormous mountains poking gently into the billowing clouds.

The geography of the land confused me. In school I had been told that Kansas was a flat, grain-producing plain. This place didn't at all resemble the Kansas of my imagination.

As I was wondering about this, an automobile loomed upon us and pulled to a dusty stop. The car carried Colorado license plates, and the driver was a gentle-looking man. He smiled at me as he welcomed us aboard his car, and I settled back easily, hoping for a long, long ride.

As we rolled along the highway, I soon found some information that cleared up my confusion. A road sign appeared with the number 40 and a Colorado emblem below it. At some time during our last train ride, we had crossed yet another state boundary and left Kansas behind. Another sign soon indicated that Denver was not far ahead. No wonder the plains had changed into such rugged terrain. We were fast approaching the mountains of the Continental Divide.

Erosion had carved massive boulders into fantastic shapes. The land was developing a scenic splendor I would learn to appreciate at a later time. Right then, the warm air blowing on me as we hummed down the highway caused me to doze, and my sleep made this portion of the trip seem quite short. I woke up, suddenly feeling alert and refreshed. We were entering the streets of a community where yet another sign told me we were in the "mile-high" city of Denver.

The kind driver pulled to the side of the street, letting us off in downtown Denver. Contrary to my expectations about our country's highest city, I was no more or less impressed by this big city than I had been by the previous cities we had recently been introduced to. It was still morning, and the air was cool and crisp. I had expected it to be rare and had thought I might find it more difficult to breathe at this altitude, but I didn't notice any difference. Everything was the same, including my hunger, and my thoughts were less about this big city than they were about how to continue our trip.

It was still rather early in the morning. We trudged along the sidewalk, aimlessly looking in store windows when, suddenly, a familiar scent drifted past us.

"Do you smell that?" David asked.

"I sure do," answered Jack.

"I do too," I said. "Smells good."

We paused in front of a worn and lonely-looking storefront. Warm oatmeal was being cooked up a flight of stairs, and a sign hanging out front identified the building as one of the homes of the Salvation Army.

The sign said there would be free food at the top of the stairs for those in need, and we certainly qualified.

"Hey, that sign says free food," I stated.

"Free!" Jack exclaimed. "I could go for that."

David said nothing. He was licking his lips in anticipation.

"Come on," I said. "Let's go see."

Hurrying up the dark stairs, which led to a narrow and dark passage, we entered a large dining area through double doors. Several wooden tables with long benches on either side were neatly arranged. At the back of the room was a long scarred counter behind which we spied a large white enamel cookstove with a wide steaming pot of oatmeal sitting on one of the burners. A man was bent over it, carefully adjusting the blue flame to a low heat to keep the porridge at a slow simmer.

Several men were sitting at tables, absently eating from heavy white bowls. One man wore an at least two-day-old beard and sported a dusty brown hat shoved back on his scraggly head. He paused a moment to glance at us, then continued scooping the porridge into his mouth.

Two others looked at us too, looked at each other, and went on eating. One of them had a heavy oversized coat on with stringy gloves that partially covered his dirty hands. The other wore a thick black sweater, which was dusty and contained several ragged holes. Others, busily eating their morning meals and oblivious to their surroundings, seemed to be completely absorbed in their own distressing thoughts.

The oatmeal smelled delicious, and once again, I experienced the anticipatory juices rising in my mouth. The man at the stove had seen us come in and beckoned us forward. We put our bedrolls in a corner of the room near a coat rack and approached a table containing the thick white bowls stacked beside a pile of tin trays and a bunch of coffee cups. Each of us helped himself to a set of utensils wrapped in a paper napkin and a large spoon, and the cook filled our bowls with the steaming creamy cereal. Finding a place at one of the long tables, we sat down to a fine breakfast. Large pitchers of hot coffee were placed on the table along with chipped blue pitchers of cold milk. Sugar and salt-and-pepper shakers had been arranged neatly on the table as well.

The cook walked over to us and handed each of us a large slice of brown toast with melted butter coloring the middle yellow. He smiled slightly, saying nothing, and returned to his station at the stove. We enjoyed our brunch and ate as though it might be our last meal.

The heavy breakfast bowls were soon empty, but we continued to sit there a while, resting and savoring our good fortune. Deciding we'd better do something to help our benefactors, we gathered our dishes and took them to a sink located beside the cooking area. On a shelf above the sink was a large green box of laundry soap and some other cleaning materials. A metal sink had some foamy warm water in it, with a large cloth lying in the middle of the partially submerged bowls. Nothing was said to us, but we began washing and drying the dishes, grateful for the opportunity to do it. Don didn't join us in helping to serve food, in cleaning up, or in any way trying to repay the generosity of the Salvation Army. I had long ago lost all respect for our adult fellow traveler.

We talked with the cook and told him of our plans to get to Los Angeles.

"California, hey," the cook remarked. "That's some distance. How you plan on getting there?"

"We've already traveled some distance to get here," Don remarked. We told the cook we hoped to ride some empty freight train boxcars, since this was the fastest manner of travel, and we wanted to cover the greatest distance possible in the shortest amount of time. The cook frowned, which intensified his next words.

"The only rail route in that direction is through what they call the "mile-long tunnel," he remarked. The friendly and helpful man described the railroad tunnel, which pierced the enormous mountain range near Mount Evans, as "dark and eerie." He had a knack with words and skillfully told his tale. He described in gruesome detail how men in the past had tried riding the rails through that particular tunnel and arrived at the other end dead. Needless to say, he was scaring us half to death. He went on to tell us that the men had died from suffocation because of the huge length of the tunnel. The engine would burn up all the air before it reached the other end.

I was so awed by what he was telling us that I failed to think of asking him about the engineer and other trainmen who regularly rode through that tunnel. We were convinced that we would surely helplessly watch one another gasping for breath and suffocate before the train could finally emerge from the dark hole. The cook smiled at our obvious concern. He must have thought he had stopped us from riding the dangerous trains.

It seemed a good idea to hang around the dining room for the day, helping out where we could while we discussed how to handle this new turn of events. We could go further south to New Mexico and then west to Los Angeles, but this could mean traveling through dangerously hot country. I had learned from my history books about early pioneers who had perished in this region. That southern route was almost entirely through desert, all the way from Arizona and California to the coast. I wasn't anxious to go by that route. The other alternative would be to head north through Utah, and then across Nevada with another desert, but the Nevada desert seemed much shorter than the one across the southern route. Don stamped about, fuming because of the quandary we were in. He provided no help.

Meanwhile, there was plenty of housework to keep us busy. During the afternoon a meeting was held in a large room, and we listened dutifully to a talk about Christian charity and the fellowship of man. After a supper of beef stew, we were shown to another large room containing several iron cots, their thin mattresses folded in half to air, I supposed. We selected some cots near each other and laid our blanket rolls on them, first using some gray blankets belonging to our hosts to cover the mattresses. We agreed that we would head north in the morning after we'd had a good night's rest and another hearty breakfast.

Jack told me later that he had worried most of that night about our passage through the Rocky Mountains. He worried also about our belongings because he was afraid someone would help themselves to our meager clothing. The only things in the world we owned were this small stack of worn clothing and the blankets we had carried across a quarter of the country. We placed a great deal of value in these few necessities, and Jack was extremely relieved the next morning to find none of our things missing. He had slept with his clothes protectively hidden under his blanket and under his slim, curled body.

The next morning, after a warm and filling breakfast, we thanked our benefactors gratefully. Our stay with the Salvation Army had made a tremendous impression on us. As we walked along the streets of Denver, I thought that even though this was such a large city, instead of being unfriendly (as were the other large cities we'd recently been in), it had given us a sense of comfort. The only thing they asked of us in return for the food and shelter they provided was that we return the kindness to others whom we might find in need. Now I felt as though I were leaving home and returning to the cold, friendless, and sometimes dangerous world again.

Again, we experienced the crisp cool air common at this altitude; but it was summer, and it would soon warm up. Our decision was to take the northern rail route, so we headed in that direction. We had been talked out of going through the long tunnel that led directly west, and we had decided against taking the scorching southern route. As far as we could see, this was our last remaining alternative.

It wasn't far to the railroad yard. We easily found an empty freight car with a tag that told us it was destined to head out in the direction we wanted to go. Climbing into the wooden cavern, we shoved aside some remnants of torn and dirty brown paper packing and made ourselves as comfortable as possible. Our timing was good because we had no sooner gotten ourselves settled than we felt the familiar bump and jar that signaled we were about to get under way. From our recent experience, we had learned to absorb this jerking and thumping, and I felt a bit pleased that this train was meeting our schedule. Within moments, we were swiftly moving through some beautiful rugged mountains. The rocks jutted from steeply sloping cliffs as the tracks wound their way through a massive canyon.

A river flowed below the rocky slopes, smashing into large boulders and sending white clouds of foam high into the sky. It was crystal clear and, except where the swift movement of the rapids obscured the view, we could clearly see rocks; and fish could also be seen in the depths of the clear blue water. Tall, straight pine trees and grotesque manzanita brush grew everywhere.

Some of the brush seemed to grow right out of these magnificent landscaped rocks. I was fascinated and filled with admiration for this beautiful sight.

The train roared as it threaded its way through the broken canyon, its freight cars swaying back and forth as we wound our way along the serpentine tracks. At times, we were able to see both the engine and the last car of the train at the same time because there were so many twists and turns through the canyon. It made me think of the fantastic hardships that must have been encountered in carving this route along the steep rocky sides of the canyon wall. Jack said he thought even a mountain goat would have found it difficult to get around in this distorted wilderness.

"Maybe so," I said. "It sure is rugged. Look over there at that huge boulder protruding out over the river. It looks as though it will fall any minute."

"Yes," Jack said, "but I bet it's been like that for many years."

"Make a nice place to jump into the river from-from that flat spot partway down." David remarked

"I can't see how you could get to the flat spot," Jack said.

"You'd probably break your neck, jumping into that river," I added.

As I looked up on the walled side of the tracks, I saw steep cliffs reaching for the sky and enormous boulders protruding sharply everywhere. On the opposite side of these tracks this vertical cliff dropped down, down until it finally crashed into the river, winding like a loosely tossed ribbon far below among the rocks. The tracks seemed to hang dangerously close to the ragged edge.

We three boys grouped around the door of the moving car, enjoying this unusual view. None of us had ever seen such a beautiful sight, and for a little while, all our hardships were forgotten in our enchantment with nature's fabulous creation. Jack and I sat there with David standing on the far side of us. The three of us were enthralled as sight after sight rolled into view, each one seeming to be more spectacular than the one before.

Suddenly the train lurched forward as it changed gears for the power necessary to continue its struggle up the precipitous incline. As I braced myself, I caught a glimpse of David in my peripheral vision. He had been caught off guard and had lost his balance. It looked as though he was about to fall forward and fly over our laps and straight out the open door. Then all I could see was the terrifying emptiness between the tracks and the floor of the yawning canyon hundreds of feet below.

David gasped in fright. Jack and I jerked around to see him seem to fall in slow motion. It all happened so fast, I hardly realized what was happening. As he was falling over our laps, we grabbed at him frantically.

Chapter 24

AWAKING FROM THE NIGHTMARE

I woke up in terror. I reached out to grab David, but all I got was a handful of empty air. Then, in the darkness, I could make out the sleeping bodies of my brothers curled up next to me. My heart was beating so hard, I felt sure it would wake them up. It took me a minute or two to realize that I had been having a nightmare about the events in our lives that led up to the terrifying experience of the previous evening. The horrible dream ended with David flying over our laps on his way out of the train just before Jack and I had caught him and pulled him back into the safety of the car. I didn't dare let myself go back to sleep as I was afraid the nightmare would return. I would like to have shared my dream with someone, but Jack and David seemed to be sleeping so peacefully that I didn't have the heart to awaken them.

When we woke up in the morning, the canyon was nowhere in sight. The train had pulled into a deserted rail yard, and we decided to make an abrupt departure so as not to take any chance of being spotted by an alert yard guard.

Nearby, a small stream sparkled in the rays of the morning sun, and we slid down the bank for a free washup. We were standing in a grassy cove not far from a highway bridge that crossed this quiet but swiftly running stream. The water slowed a little as it ran through a pool by our cove. Water grasses waved gently near us, and we saw bait fish darting here and there in the clearness of the pool.

When we had finished washing, we caught the smell of a nearby campfire wafting toward us on the light morning breeze. Of course, we quickly decided to investigate. Over toward the bridge, a man was sitting on a large rock watching a large can set over a few sticks burning in a small pit. Perched precariously on some flat rocks was what looked like a gallon-size fruit can, its label burned off. The water was already boiling, and the man was peeling and slicing some potatoes into it. He looked up as he heard us approach, and I got the distinct impression that he was not too happy at the idea of having guests for dinner. We were obviously hoboes on the road as he was, and sharing his meal had not been part of his plan for the day. He only grunted at us as we drew near. We gathered some nearby kindling to add to his fire. Our gift, and perhaps our age, apparently touched him, and he grudgingly offered us a little of his potato soup.

The soup was bland, though, with some slight flavor that indicated that the old man had added other vegetables besides the potatoes to the boiling water. I was grateful enough just to feel the warmth of the soup spread through my belly to my limbs. It was such a comforting feeling to fill up what had seemed like a vast emptiness and to assuage our permanent hunger. The liquid had a slight metallic taste, but I figured it came from the can he was using as a pot.

Because the road across the bridge appeared to have very little traffic on it, we decided to stay here in this small hobo camp. While Don was napping under a nearby tree, we boys swapped stories with our benefactor, listening with awe to some of the tales the old man spun. He told of seeing a man crushed under the enormous wheels of one train because of his own carelessness.

"Yep," he said as we listened intently, "the young fool tried to hop onto a freight car that was traveling far too fast.

"He lost his footing, I guess," the old man continued. "Slung him right under those iron wheels. Didn't hardly have time to holler."

"Was it bloody?" David asked.

"Yep, shore were," the man answered.

A chill ran through my body. Jack and I looked at each other. We didn't say anything. The old man also told us that trains passing nearby would leave at about two in the afternoon and that outside of town there was a small grade, which caused the heavily laden freight trains to slow to a dragging pace. If we intended to continue our travels by rail, he said, we would be better off to catch the boxcar on this rise or miss it altogether, because only at this point would the train be going slow enough for it to be safe to jump in.

"Shore hate to see another mess, much less three," he remarked.

"You taking that train?" Jack asked.

"Nope," he answered. "I'm not going anywhere particular for a while."

It was approaching noon, and we were lying about, resting. Suddenly, even to my own surprise, I became violently sick. Every muscle in my body ached, as if I had been beaten, and a blinding headache descended crushingly so that I lost all control of myself. I vomited and retched until I was totally exhausted, afraid I was going to die and nearly wishing that I would.

This was the first time on the journey that any of us had become sick; we thought it must have been from the potato soup we had eaten a little earlier. Though it seemed strange, and fortunate, that no on else got sick. I suspect it may have been caused by the can I had used to hold my portion of the soup.

"That can wasn't too clean," I said. "I guess it had some bad specks in it."

"You all right?" Jack asked with concern.

David was anxiously listening for my answer.

"Yes," I answered. "I feel fine now that I got that rot out of me." "Boy, that was bad," I added.

The old hobo thought I had food poisoning too. He got some of the charcoal from the campfire embers and made a black mixture from warm water, which he insisted I drink. I swallowed as much of the dreadful stuff as I could. And I guess it worked, for immediately I vomited the whole mess, cleaning my stomach. Once my stomach was empty, I began to feel better, but it was quite some time before I had any enthusiasm about eating again.

"There, I told ya so," said the old man. "Works every time." He chuckled in satisfaction.

When, in a few hours, it was time to leave, we felt it best to find a good vantage point at the rise of the hill along the westward trails where we had been told the trains would slow to a crawl. I certainly didn't feel much like rushing about anyway, and it seemed wise to use every possible advantage presented to us. Finding some tumbleweeds near the tracks, we fashioned ourselves some crude chairs and sat down to wait. Although it seemed we waited for quite a long time, the trains were running on schedule. Eventually, a very long freight train approached, hardly appearing to move at all as it struggled up the rise just outside the train yard.

"Keep low," I whispered.

We all clung to the ground near the large bushes shielding us.

"What are we whispering for?" David whispered.

"I don't know," I chuckled. "With all the noise that engine's making, no one could possibly hear us."

The train didn't get much of a running start for the hill, and as the old man had promised, it was easy for us to throw our gear onto a passing boxcar and scramble up after it. It wasn't until after we'd jumped aboard the first available car on the train that I looked out and saw people pouring from the brush to follow our example. I had thought we were practically alone, and now people were literally springing from every tumbleweed and gully. This freight train would be carrying a considerably greater weight than the engineer could possibly have realized.

As we were preparing our bed at the front of the car, a suitcase was tossed through the door, rapidly followed by a well-dressed man and woman. I was quite surprised, but I guess I shouldn't have been. In these days, it wasn't unusual for a person with good clothes to have little else and to be in need of transportation. I tried to guess the purpose of their journey, and in my romantic imagination, I wondered whether they might be eloping. I continued to watch them out of the corner of my eye, and they continued to sit firmly and silently on their suitcases and remain that way all the night through, I suppose.

Early in the morning, we were rudely awakened by a roar from a man standing at the door of the car. He held a mean-looking club in his fist and was ordering everyone out, his bellow fairly setting the cool morning air afire. Sitting up on our makeshift bed, I saw the well-dressed couple stand up and gather their suitcases and coats. Still not a word was heard from them; they left immediately.

We told the club-wielding man we would be gone as quickly as we could get our bedrolls together. He growled something indistinguishable and continued down the line of cars, rousting everyone else off the train. We started putting our things together, taking our time at it. But by the time all our ropes were tied and we were ready to go, the train gave a sudden lurch that sent us rolling back to the other side of the car. Two or three heavy bumps, and the long freight train was under way again—with us still aboard. And since it continued in our direction, we just sat tight and enjoyed the ride. This portion of the trip, the train sped us through many small towns. Telephone poles along the railroad right-of-way were a blur as we passed through without seeming to slow down at all. I fell into my old hypnotic trance, and it seemed as though the poles were reproaching me for traveling this way. A steady *swish-swish-swish* sound as the poles sped past.

At crossroads the warning bells would be clanging, the sound rising as we approached and then falling away into the distance as we passed. It was a weird experience because, from having heard the bells so many times in the past, I knew the sound didn't really change at all. It would be many years before I learned this was called the Doppler effect. At that time it just seemed to create a sad and mournful atmosphere, lacking only a chilling downpour to make it complete.

I began to notice how run-down the buildings in these towns appeared, and I thought about the families who lived in them, struggling to survive the terrible hardships so many people were experiencing in the aftermath of the Depression. This was one of the places where the results of these hardships were obvious. The fences between the houses and the tracks were in desperate need of repair, or they had fallen down altogether. Old automobiles, rusty and scarred, lay about in many backyards—some with their hoods up where, most likely, a would-be repairman had given up in disgust and just walked away. Or maybe the cars had been scalped for parts to keep another car running.

Mongrel dogs yapped incessantly—whether at cats or at the passing train, I wasn't sure—and the roads on the outskirts of these towns were usually unpaved, or they were tarred lightly but with potholes and ruts so deeply gouged that I wondered how a car could possibly navigate along them. All the children I saw playing in the sad backyards or streets were dirty. I couldn't stop thinking wistfully that, at least, they had a home to go to at the end of the day.

Around noontime, the screech of iron wheels grabbing iron rails and the sight of more and more sets of tracks spreading out like an outstretched hand signaled that we were arriving at another rail yard. We seemed to be quite a distance from any city. Many long lines of boxcars had been left on sidings, their engines now used to transport other cars. Such was now the fate of our train, and it was time for us also to leave it behind.

Other than a few small, securely locked wooden sheds, we didn't see much else in this rail yard except a weathered sign announcing that the city in the distance was Salt Lake City. We had no desire to see its sights. We were hungry and thirsty, and as the sun climbed higher and higher, it was getting hotter and hotter. A warm west wind caressed the lonely rails as well as the stranded cars, but it didn't offer us enough relief to keep us from praying that our wait for the next ride wouldn't be long. Despite our hunger and thirst, our primary concern was to hear the approach of an engine to hook up with some of these cars and continue us on our way west.

"Do you think we'll have to wait long?" Jack asked.

"I'm not sure," I answered. "I wonder if today is Sunday. The place sure seems deserted."

"There are plenty of empty boxcars," David commented.

"Yea," Jack said, "but not much good if they aren't going anywhere."

"I'm thirsty," David said absently.

"Me too," Jack said. "A little hungry too."

I looked about the lonely rail yard. The freight cars gave me the impression that they had all gone to sleep in the hot sun. I felt a little irritated. I was impatient at having to wait like this for the unknown.

As the hours wore on, our thirst became acute. Our mouths were longing for moisture, and we were dripping with perspiration. Our desire for water became intense. We'd become more or less used to skipping meals now and then, but water was something we couldn't do without. Our minds became preoccupied with the thought of finding something to drink and some shade so we could get out of the sun. I wished we had saved those jars of water we'd had earlier, but we had been carelessly wasteful and were now learning another lesson the hard way. We tried to take advantage of some shade by getting under the boxcars; but the air under there wasn't stirring, so it wasn't much help. It was so stuffy that we imagined we were in a gigantic oven.

Then, while shading my eyes from the hot rays of the sun, I spotted small drips of water coming from wooden spouts on the refrigerated cars. An opening to that particular type of car had been provided to allow the melting ice a runoff place. It was barely more than one drop at a time, but seeing it added to my need and desire for a drink and caused me to involuntarily lick my parched lips. I walked over to the enticing drip and held a rag I used as a handkerchief under the spout, letting the drops soak into the cloth. When the handkerchief was soaking wet, I used it to dampen my lips and wash my sweating face.

"Hey, that looks good," Jack exclaimed.

"Boy," I said, "it's better than nothing. Try it."

Jack and David followed suit, and by this means, we were able to slack our thirst to a small degree at least. The water tasted a bit odd, having picked up some of the flavor of the wooden spout; but despite its strange taste and odor, it was very much appreciated by all of us.

"Tastes like it came from 'the old wooden bucket,'" I said.

"That's all right," Jack replied.

Jack soaked his undershirt and put it back on, exclaiming over and over how good it felt. So David and I did likewise, and we too experienced a feeling of relief—a temporary one anyway. The dry heat soon had our shirts dry again and returned us to our former sweltering condition.

Chapter 25

SALT LAKE CITY:

THE MORMONS TO THE RESCUE

As time passed, we became more and more convinced that we couldn't wait around this furnace of a rail yard much longer. We saw no indication that an engine might be forthcoming or that any of the trains would be moving in the near future, so we gathered our gear and began a trudge toward the city far off in the distance. Maybe we could find a ride on a highway, wherever that was. It was imperative that we continue our forward motion. To merely sit and wait would mean the end for us.

We walked to a major highway leading toward the city. A large sign told us it was U.S. Highway 40. As we walked, we discussed the possibilities for our next move. Thinking that the best bet was going to be to hitchhike again, we stayed on Route 40.

Approaching the downtown section of the city, we found ourselves surrounded by tall buildings. Because of our prior experience with big cities, we weren't saddened that the scurrying crowds took no notice of these bedraggled people: us.

We weren't the least bit interested in the buildings or the scenery, but our eyes were caught by a sign on one building, which indicated that welfare was available within. People were straggling through the doors, and seeing that others were taking advantage of the opportunity gave us the courage to go in. After all, we had nothing to lose and perhaps a free meal to gain, we thought. So we followed some other people through the doors. Inside was a large room with what appeared to be discarded rows of wooden theater seats scattered at various places. Along one end of the room were scarred and discolored desks and tables, with a person sitting on one side of a desk asking questions and a person seated on the other side of the desk answering them. Behind each of the people being questioned was a line of people waiting their turn to be interviewed. The folks in the lines looked at least as bad off as we did, with clothing that was worn and tattered, some of them even barefoot.

We joined one of the lines, and when our turn came, I listened carefully as Don answered the questions put to him. Because he was afraid there would be no help if they thought we were just passing through town, he said we had come to Salt Lake City to stay. I don't think the man at the desk was fooled one bit, but he didn't really seem to care one way or the other. He filled out his forms with our names, ages, and general information about us; he seemed to be interested only in the data and not in us as human beings. I guess he had to process so many needy and woebegone people in the continual lines that he had become hardened in order to be able to keep doing his job.

Our interviewer handed us several different tickets and instructed as to the location of a hotel, a grocery store, and a café. The tickets could be used at those places and would take care of our immediate needs. We were welcome to the community. He told us to return to this hall the next morning for instructions about how to find work and a more permanent place to stay. We learned that all this kindness was provided by the Latter Day Saints, or Mormons, of Salt Lake City.

After leaving the hall, we looked up the café that we had been directed to. We took prompt advantage of the café tickets. As soon as we walked in, we could see that the place could use a good cleaning. The floor needed to be swept, and the yellowish walls were streaked with grease and grime. We slid into a worn booth from where we had a view of the whole disreputable looking place. Our booth had knife slits in the upholstery, some of which had been patched with different colored pieces of plastic tape, but cotton still protruded from many places as though the owners simply couldn't keep up.

Handing the waiter the café ticket, he left to get our order. Apparently, a standard fare for the tickets. We really didn't care about the quality of either the restaurant or the food. It was the quantity that mattered to us. The waiter brought each of us bowls of soup. We wolfed down some watery vegetable soup that was hot and tasty. That was followed by meat loaf, mashed potatoes, and peas and rolls. Coffee and milk were also available. Every bit of it was delicious. We stuffed ourselves and were thankful for every bite of everything offered. I saw in the menu that the meat loaf dinner was a dollar and fifty cents. This included the coffee or milk. I was impressed by the amount of money the church must be putting out, and for so many people!

Following the directions given at the welfare office, we located the aged and musty-smelling hotel. A clerk who hadn't shaved that morning appeared from behind some dingy curtains when we walked in. He hid a smelly cigar stub under the counter and shoved a book register toward us to sign, taking the hotel tickets from Don. He handed Don a key and directed us to our room. After walking down a dimly lit hallway, we found the room number inked onto one of the doors. Entering, we saw a small bare room with two large ancient beds and a single dresser. The dirty windows were covered with curtains made from sheets that had once been white but were now a dingy gray. We were to share a bathroom with the occupants of two other rooms. It contained a pungent-smelling commode with yellow dirt clinging to it and a tin shower. Both the bedroom and the bathroom had a musty odor, but in spite of everything, this looked like heaven to us.

We each showered, using the tiny wrapped bars of soap provided by the hotel. We then washed our clothes in the cracked sink in the corner of our bedroom. We were able to hang our wet clothes on the foot of the brass bedstead. Presentable at last, we went to the allocated small grocery nearby and began selecting the food permitted to us by the last of our tickets. Mostly we chose small canned goods, things which wouldn't easily spoil. Our stomachs were full now, but we were thinking of the days to come. In addition to the food items, I selected a can opener, figuring we would be needing it.

"This is great," Jack exclaimed.

"Yeah," David said. "Look at all the food we can get. Can we get some cookies too?"

"Sure," I answered.

"Maybe we should stay here," David thought out loud.

"Heck no," Jack said angrily. "We've got to get to California and find Mom."

"Yes, we do," I added. "And while you're at it, get each of us a bar of that candy."

Back at the hotel, we spread our riches on the bed and divided them evenly among us so that no one would have too much to carry, and then we climbed under the sheets for our first night's sleep in a real bed since we had left Cincinnati. How long ago that seemed! I slept well that night. Thank you, Salt Lake City!

Chapter 26

CROSSING THE NEVADA DESERT

Staying in the generous city of Salt Lake had never been our intent, so we didn't return to the welfare hall the next morning. Instead, we headed straight out to the railroad yard. In spite of our gratitude to the Latter Day Saints, we hadn't lost our driving purpose of getting to Los Angeles as quickly as possible. I would have been willing to bet we weren't the only ones who took advantage of the good graces of that fine church. At least, it made me feel better to believe that.

The yard was buzzing with activity, so we quickly located a freight tagged for Reno. We remembered our terrible thirst of the day before, and I knew that between Salt Lake City and Reno lay a desert that this train would in all likelihood be traversing. This would make it the hottest part of our journey thus far. There was a small wooden building of some kind alongside the tracks, close to where freight trains' boxcars were. In front of the building was a carton with empty jars with lids. To guard against again suffering such thirst as we had before, we took some of the jars, washed them from a nearby water faucet, and filled them with water for our journey. Then we climbed aboard the empty boxcar. We made ourselves comfortable in the shade the car provided. I recalled reading that desert prospectors carried canteens, which allowed their water to be kept cool by evaporation. Knowing that blowing air over a wet body causes this cooling by evaporation, we placed our water jars near the open car doors where the moving air would blow directly on them.

"Is Reno a big city too?" asked David.

"I don't know," I answered. "I have read and heard about it, but I've never been there."

It wasn't long into the trip that we found we had made a drastic mistake. I hadn't accounted for the fact that the blowing air would be hot and dry and would have an unfortunate reaction on the water in our jars. We were about to learn yet another lesson. The jars should have been covered with wet rags.

Meanwhile, we settled down to enjoy the next leg of our trip.

The tracks had been laid at the edge of the Great Salt Lake, making for an impressive view. Sparkling salt deposits lined the shores, but the water in the shallows was very rusty in color due to the thickening of beds of salt as the water evaporated in the hot sun. It seemed odd how the rusty water could change into sparkling white crystals of table salt.

We saw an industrial area along the shoreline, probably a plant for retrieving the salt that would eventually be found on dining room tables. Some unpainted wooden buildings scattered along the shore looked ancient. It made me wonder what this climate would do to the human skin.

Our train sped on, replacing the landscape of the lake with dry brush and cactus. The soil was dirty, whitish, and sandy—tightly packed in places and loose in others. The area was almost completely barren, wide areas of nothing but sand, so abandoned and foreboding. But even here, we found interesting things to engage our interest and to watch for. Large jackrabbits leapt swiftly away from the metallic noise of the train. Desert plants swished by as we rushed westward.

"Where do you think those rabbits get their food and water?" Jack asked.

"I don't know," I answered. "Probably, they can live from those dry-looking weeds out there. Can't figure where they'd get water, though."

Jack nodded in agreement.

We lay back against our blanket rolls and were soon lulled to sleep.

My nap was brought to an abrupt halt by the thump of those huge iron wheels rattling over the joints in the rails, and I heard my brothers moaning in their sleep. Their clothes were soaked with perspiration in the now-sweltering boxcar, and mine were too. I moved quickly over to the jars to get a drink. Reaching out for one of the jars, I realized to my utter horror that the hot air blowing across the jars had acted like a stove, and the water was almost too hot to touch. I had forgotten that part of the preparation to cool water was to place a wet cloth over the tops of the jars to provide the evaporation action.

The jars were so hot, I had to use my shirt to lift them into the shaded part of the car. Then I dipped my shirt into the water to wipe my face and experienced the same cooling action we had discovered earlier in the trip when Jack had wet his tee shirt. It worked even though the water was so hot that I had to wait for it to cool off a bit before I could touch it. Jack and David, waking, followed my example.

"Wow," Jack exclaimed. "This water is hot."

"Yeah, we could have made tea this way," David said. "If we had the tea bags."

"The wet rags feel cool, though," Jack noted.

We were, at least momentarily, more comfortable. Once again, we had paid a high price to learn a lesson. We sure were paying our tuition in the School of Hard Knocks. My memories of this trip across the Nevada Desert are not pleasant. In later years, I would come to appreciate the special beauty of this area; but at this time it was just miserable, hot, and ugly. I had anticipated a beautiful desert of white sand, but this panoramic landscape was a dry prairie broken by deep cracks in the brush-strewn ground. What at one time must have been creeks, with water eroding the rocky soil, were now only empty trenches, bone dry. The hills were occasionally rolling, but every-so-often they formed steep, rocky plateaus. Some of the sides had fallen raggedly away, enormous boulders cascading down to lie at the foot of the hill. Other plateaus looked as though they had been blown apart by some sudden catastrophic force.

Now I think that this desert has a unique beauty that I was in no mood to appreciate at the time. I was just too miserable. The brush struck me as weird—generally brown, gray, or white-dry occasionally a greenish color, and often seeming to grow right out of the rocks. Cacti were everywhere, and I was surprised to see so many different types and sizes. Nature couldn't seem to make up her mind which kind was best in this fearsome, lonely land. What a terrible experience the earlier covered wagon people had to have endured. At least, I knew what was on the other side.

It had been only a year ago, while traveling through Southern California and Arizona on our way to Cincinnati, that we had seen tall thick trees reminiscent of cacti. Here, the same trees were mostly short and stumpy-looking. Some were slender with a thick coat of thin needles making them look as though they were wearing fur coats. Many of the cacti had succumbed to the ravages of heat and dryness in this hostile desert. They lay in grotesque patterns as though they had died in agony.

Once we watched a jackrabbit, who had been hopping from one small shady spot to another, freeze in its tracks and remain frozen, its ears pointing straight up to the hot blue sky.

"Look at that rabbit," I said.

Jack said, "It probably thinks it's fooling this terrible iron monster, which has caught it out in the open."

"Yes," I said, laughing at Jack's imagination.

We quickly learned yet another lesson. It was best to lie as still as possible during this wearying desert portion of the trip so as not to use any extra energy. What little of that which we'd had seemed to be drained out of us by the oppressive heat, even when we didn't move at all. Our energy oozed from our pores, and I became alarmed at the amount of sweat that covered us. We looked as though we had just come in out of a downpour, although it was obvious that it hadn't rained in these parts in months, if not years.

Our sweat and the dust blowing in began to mix, and in my imagination, we looked like broiled pigs. Jack and David sought relief by sleeping as much as possible, but I wasn't as lucky as they were, and I only managed to doze from time to time. The sweltering heat kept waking me up. It was difficult to breathe with the terrible heat pressing in on us so heavily. I began to wonder if we were going to survive. To wet our dry lips and throats, we took sips from our water jars. Thank God we had that much.

Occasionally the train would stop, but the stops were brief and offered no respite from the broiling sun. Stopping just made things worse because the air didn't move. Each time the train stopped in the middle of this desert, I wondered if it was going to drop us off at a siding. We ate some of our "Mormon rations," savoring especially the juice we had chosen at the Salt Lake City grocery store. Eventually, the sun began to sink in the western sky, and the dusk brought with it a slight lowering of the temperature.

Just as we were beginning to relish this change, full night was upon us. It came with a sudden surge of bone-chilling cold. We were astonished that the desert didn't retain any of the awesome heat of the day. We huddled close together in our blankets, barely able to keep warm. We marveled at how fragile the human body is. We came to a realization now that just a small change in temperature determined our comfort or discomfort, sometimes our very lives. We did survive that terrible ride, though, thanks mostly to the mind-blanking numbness of sleep.

Nevada did not have many small towns in the desert areas. I looked forward to seeing what the city of Reno looked like.

Chapter 27

RELIEF IN RENO

It was a shock to come upon the city so abruptly. There were no warning suburbs, only the surprise of bleak desert one moment and modern buildings the next—an amazing juxtaposition on this age-old, useless prairie. That wide, white, barren land was finally behind us; and our joy, as the Reno train yard appeared, was boundless. There was sure to be a cool drink of water somewhere nearby. I was so glad we hadn't chosen to take the southern route out of Denver. If we had, our suffering would have lasted so much longer.

We couldn't believe the richness of the buildings! Moments ago, we'd been in a bleak and barren desert; and the next moment, we found ourselves in a fairyland. A carnival of bright lights and color flashing everywhere. The train slowed to a walk. From the safety of our perch in the Southern Pacific train we were riding, we watched the crowds of people. Despite the fact that this looked like a circus town, people didn't seem to be happy. I thought maybe the sad condition of our Depression-weary country had affected even these residents of such a joyful-looking place. I could find no other reason to account for all the long faces I saw.

Now the railway tracks crossed a roadway with the familiar clanging of its warning bell. A short time later, we entered what a sign, stretched from one side of a street to the other, told us was "The Biggest Little City in the West." The train continued to slow its pace, providing a good vantage point from which to view the exciting scene. Then off in the distance to the left of the car, I saw a river.

"Look, a river," Jack exclaimed just then.

"Yeah," I said, savoring the thought of its coolness.

"Think there's any fish in it?" David asked.

"It's big enough," Jack answered.

"Where there's water, there's fish," I remarked jokingly.

When our train finally ground to a halt, we fell wearily from the car, longing for the water we had seen dripping from an old rusty faucet across the way; bright green moss and grass gleefully spread over the wet boundary of the soaked earth around it. Unmindful of the curious taste, we drank our fill and then washed as much of the greasy dust away as we could. Soaking our head felt so much better.

Shade at the side of one of the sheds in the rail yard provided us a place to sprawl, and I was relieved at the speed with which our bodies recovered. Our rapid recuperation was due in part to the shade and the water, but a small meal of some of the canned goods from Salt Lake City was a significant help as well. We opened our cans with the opener we had bought back at that grocery store in Salt Lake City, but it was clear it wasn't meant to be used often. It was flimsy and clumsy to use. I had a devil of a time opening a can of pork and beans. Jack contributed some doughnuts, and David provided a can of peaches from his stock. These things, together with canned milk diluted with water, were the basis for a feast for us.

Satisfied and refreshed, we lay back in the shade near the shed. We got some sleep, which was considerably more renewing to our spirits and bodies than the drugged sleep of the trip through the desert. We savored it all: the food, the coolness, the rest. The worst of our trip across Nevada's mesas was behind us. I made a little prayer of thanks. The gay city was just across the way, and we were at peace. We spent that night in a draw, an old water runoff located behind the railroad shed.

I woke up at sunrise—the eastern sky yellow and orange in the distance, the breeze cool, and the air crisp. I marveled at the curiousness of the weather in this state. Could it be so swelteringly hot during the day and downright frigid at night? The geology seemed to absorb the heat totally, and yet was unable to retain it once the sun had fallen into the west. How strange.

Chapter 28

FROM THE PRAIRIES TO THE MOUNTAINS

As usual, we wanted to be on our way as soon as possible; so after a sparse breakfast, we investigated this day's possibilities for western travel. Again, luck was with us, for we quickly found an empty gravel car tagged for Oakland, California. An exhilarating thrill swept through me, as I read those magic letters: C-A-L-I-F-O-R-N-I-A! This was the car we'd been watching for during the whole weary journey!

We believed that the trip from Reno to Oakland would be accomplished in daylight hours, so an open freight car would do as well as a closed one this time. A climb up the rusty ladder and down the other side put us on the floor of a battered and beaten relic of a car. The hard stones of many cascading cargoes had left it dented and bulging, but we made ourselves as comfortable as possible, happy in the assurance that the end of this trip to California was in sight. I remembered our very first rail-riding experience when we had shuttled around the train yard, going nowhere. The frustration of that time was still with me, and I felt a chill go through my body as I wondered if we had really read this car's tag correctly.

It was a foolish fear, I knew. We were veterans of the road now. We had met and conquered many dangers and hazards, and although we still had more traveling to do before we reached our destination, I knew in my bones that we could not be beaten now. I shook off the momentary fear. I had found confidence through our experiences and was certain we could overcome any obstacle that might yet be in our path.

My meditation was broken by the familiar jolt and violent shaking that signaled the coupling of the train to an engine. We felt another backbreaking jar that broke loose the brakes of the car, overcoming their rigidity from standing so long in one place; we were soon swaying along the tracks past the brightly lit city.

Now, from my position in the open car, I saw high, snow-covered peaks looming ahead. The final big obstacle to our goal was in sight, the high Sierra Range. I recalled the fantasies I'd had when I lived in Los Angeles, when I'd dreamed of these fabulous mountains, when—though I had never touched snow—I would imagine jumping into hundreds of feet of snowbanks without injury. I had also dreamed of the wondrous things that must be on the other side of that high mountain range.

My thoughts must have been something like those of early explorers, except that in my boyhood dreams I didn't appreciate the coldness and dampness of snow—the sudden chill and the stiffening muscles that went along with the beauty of this white, cotton-appearing stuff.

I had learned differently in Cincinnati, where I saw snow ugly with grit and grime and had suffered the teeth-chattering dampness and cold. I dreaded the thought of going through such misery again and turned my thoughts to the warm California climate toward which we were heading.

We were moving in the direction of my dreams. The ragged and barren plains of Nevada were now behind us in the east. The country we were now passing through was far from barren. Many animals thrived in the chopped hills and on the wide brush-covered plains. We saw a coyote sneak around some boulders and many jackrabbits and other squirrel-like rodents among the rocks. We were certain that snakes must abound in this rocky land, though we did not see any. Those weird flat-topped plateaus with no trees other than scrub were quickly left behind.

In the distance I could see white smoke, or steam, rising from small hills to the south of Reno. The rolling ground seemed alive as steam spewed from mysterious spots. I thought that early pioneers must have found that another fear to add to their growing lists of frightening unknowns in this wild country. Could this be the entrances to Satan's hell?

I then saw a river, which I later learned was the Truckee River, flowing not far from the route of the train tracks, carving a tree-lined scar across the land. The railroad tracks carefully followed the twists and turns of the river. Obviously, this had been the simplest way in which to lay the tracks.

The approaching mountains seemed to grow taller the closer we came to them, and the trees fewer. The mountainsides were studded with enormous cracked or broken granite boulders, larger than any we had previously seen. There appeared to be several canyons where the folds of the high range molded together, all of this made more beautiful by the early morning dew, which seemed to add an exhilarating sparkle to the whole scene.

Our train roared through another city, whistling its wailing cry as we passed the highway crossings, the gates safely down and the warning bells clanging an accompaniment to the music of the train. After a short while, I felt the long train slowing and, looking over the side of our open car, I saw that we had begun to climb a long steep grade up the mountain slope. The engine was pulling around a wide curve, and I could see both ends of the train as it struggled up and around the banked, sweeping turn. There were, in fact, two engines puffing steam and bellowing smoke as they worked to pull us up and over these high sierras. At the far end of the train, where normally a red caboose tagged along, there was yet a third engine, pushing as though to guarantee our success in this seemingly impossible climb.

We rose higher and higher as we moved deeper into the mountains. It appeared that the entire world was suddenly mountains, each range interlaced with another range for as far as I could see. Great cliffs and projections of granite surrounded us. Towering above were boulders threatening to break loose and crash down on this insignificant intruder of a train at any moment. If one of them did fall, it would destroy the whole train and wipe out a great length of track. It didn't make me feel any more secure to see scores of smaller rock lying by the track where they had tumbled.

The Truckee River was crashing its way among large rocks far below in the canyon, the sparkling clear water happily dancing in the air from one large boulder to another. The tracks we followed were carved through and around, as well as past, tremendous boulders dotted with sparse brush and trees. At times, the roadbed clung precariously to the steep, wild cliffs. On one side of the tracks, the ledge suddenly dropped far below in a dizzy rock-strewn fall.

A curious wooden structure had been built along the mountainside in a fairly straight line. I believed it to be some type of water-carrying device, bringing the snowmelt from the mountains to the towns below in the valley. This was indicated moments later by water escaping gleefully though a crack in a long waterfall.

Where there was soil to be seen, some type of yellow plant painted the landscape. Its colors mixed well with the green of the pine and brush, adding another kind of beauty to the mountainside. The wrinkled appearance of the endless ranges, together with the color of the plant life, gave the landscape the look of a gigantic rumpled, unmade bed.

Across the canyon was a winding highway climbing toward the clouds. It must have been very narrow, for I could see a large bus creeping down to Nevada and a car laboring up the hill in the western direction. As they passed one another, the bus seemed to be right at the edge of the road, while the car was practically glued to the vertical mountainside. It surely looked like a frightening route to drive, this steep winding road, with its many S curves and few straightaways following the natural contours of the mountain.

Our train slowly continued its upward climb to California, now passing some burned streaks of dead pine covering entire hillsides—mute and ugly evidence of some past fire or disease. Within the shelter of the mountains were several valleys, wide and open, which must have been attractive to early settlers as they moved westward. The outcroppings of tall pine trees would have provided them with material for building their log cabins. The Truckee River and other swift streams would have provided the assurance of water year round.

The whole world around us now was comprised of mountains and cliffs. As the train sliced through a pass, we saw abrupt changes in the panoramic scenery. Massive pines painted in light and dark shades of green glowed up and away as far as we could see. Some oak and other greenery, together with a lot of brush, filled the areas between these magnificent trees. But mostly, these slopes were covered by the vast pine forests.

The climate was changing from the dry warm air of the Nevada daytime to the cooler and much more pleasant atmosphere of the mountains. The odor of pine in the air was heavy enough to cover up the stench of the railroad. How refreshing to our train-weary noses. Distant hillside valleys sparkled with beautiful lakes, promising a cool peacefulness. The abrasive noises of our train had no effect on the quiet of the water, twinkling in the sunshine.

Frequent and sudden turns brought varying sights from Alpine-like pastures to the rugged cliffs and huge granite outcroppings. The hill would drop suddenly far below and then be blocked by another mountain. Once, I saw three deer with magnificent antlers staring at us as we passed. They showed no sign of fear, but were poised to bolt for the woods at the first sign of danger. Other wildlife we saw included a thick woolly porcupine lumbering along a narrow trail, not appearing to notice the metal monster passing loudly near his territory. I guessed the animals were familiar with the occasional passing of trains through their land.

We felt the triumph of Mother Nature as we screamed over the summit where a wooden sign proclaimed our elevation as 7,329 feet. On the western slopes, the trees thickened to forests of pine and tall cedar. There were, occasionally, many different hardwood trees too. The pines grew taller and taller, and fewer dead limbs lay about or clung precariously to the tall tree trunks ready to fall on an unsuspecting hiker. Apparently, water was more readily available on this, the western side of the Sierras.

The rugged pines grew in all sorts of unlikely spots. I saw some that seemed to grow directly from the barren granite rock. We traveled through one valley whose entire length was of solid granite, which—had I had the privilege—I would have named Granite Pass. I noticed a sign along the track, which identified the area as Big Bend. The name probably reflected the location of a wide curve in the Yuba River far below us. The river on this side of the mountain slopes flowed in the opposite direction and was given a different name from the eastern Truckee River.

High above the broken rocks and dense forests, I saw an eagle floating gently in the open sky, searching for a meal of mice or any small game he could spy. Suddenly he plunged down the western slopes, which brought me to the sudden appreciation that we were finally in California. We drank in the fantastic beauty. I marveled at the grandeur, finding it hard to remember the hardships we had so recently endured to get here.

I was absorbed by the forests of tall pine, wanting to hold on to the feeling they evoked forever. Reality was lost to me. I was no longer impoverished, but rich with the splendor of my surroundings. I needed to know that I mattered, that somebody somewhere in the world cared, and the great woods seemed to fill my need. The disillusionment of my real world dropped away.

Though I knew the mountains would soon disappear also, they had filled me with a renewed promise of the goodness of life. Sometimes I had felt I was drowning with lead boots on, suffering utter despair. It seemed I'd been manipulated and was powerless to do anything about it. Now, these glorious mountains had renewed and refreshed my spirit. The enormity of this Sierra Mountain Range promised better ways to live and certain success, so long as I never gave up.

Jack, David, and I agreed. We felt welcomed home by the arms of these wonderful mountains, almost as a mother welcomes her lost child. Sooner than we would have liked, we were descending down, down, down. Manzanita bushes began to be mixed in with the beloved pines and oaks. Red California clay became more and more apparent as we passed through a region know as Grass Valley. We had to look behind us to find the mountains. There was still a lot of rock, but it was a different type—more fragile appearing than granite.

We were still thick in the pine forest, but more and more of the trees we saw were black oaks. The acorns from the ancient-looking white oaks towering over much of the land had been a staple in the diet of the Indians of old California.

"Would be nice to have some nuts to snack on," I said.

"Yeah," David said, as he observed the view.

"I'd like to have an apple," Jack commented.

"Yeah," David remarked again. "Or maybe a peach."

The trees became scarcer as we entered the Sacramento Valley. The rugged wilderness turned into rolling hills, but off in the far distance, I could just make out another mountain range. Those must surely be the coastal mountains. Farms and homes became more numerous along our route, pleasant homes sitting primly amid neatly ordered fields. The sky was clear blue, the sun shining with increasing heat as we wound down into the valley. Old buildings—sun bleached nearly white—flicked by, and the pungent odor of sun-dried grass permeated the air.

I thought at first the train would stop in Sacramento, but it appeared to roll, straight as an arrow, right through this part of the city. Some of the buildings here were of the "on the other side of the tracks" type. I could see a much larger domed building in the distance, which most likely was the state's capitol building. After passing over a river, the tracks turned in a wide curve. The train slowed considerably but slowly continued to crawl as it passed through a large railroad yard.

"Are we stopping?" David asked.

"No. Not yet, anyway. Just relax," I answered.

I really wasn't sure what the train was going to do. I soon saw a large bridge ahead. As we passed over a big river, I saw a sign identifying it as the Sacramento River. As soon as we got on the western side of the river, the train began to pick up speed. Buildings became scarce once again. The landscape opened up to some form of watershed area. A few cows were quietly grazing on the lush green grass. We continued westward, closing in on those coastal mountain ranges.

Stockton, Oakland, the Pacific Ocean—wouldn't be far away now. I felt the excitement welling up within me, even though I realized we still had several hundred miles between us and Los Angeles.

Now the rows of eucalyptus trees carefully planted as windbreaks by farmers began to appear. They were so typical of the California I knew and loved. It occurred to me, watching the lines of eucalyptus, that it might have been better to have planted food-bearing trees to protect the fields. Probably, this was because food was almost always the number one thing on my mind these days. It was obvious that the eucalyptus was the only tree tall enough to serve the purpose of windbreaks.

Speeding on, passing crossings at highways and small back-country roads, we paid little attention to the details of our surroundings until, suddenly, in a small town, I was shocked to see a man hanging from the overhanging rafters of one of the buildings. A second look brought me to the realization that it was only a dummy, hung for an advertisement of some kind. California goes in for some bizarre advertising gimmicks, but my double take proved worthwhile.

Paralleling the tracks was a winding highway with only a few cars moving along it. I was pleased to notice that we were moving a great deal faster than those automobiles. Our engine wailed its mournful cry again as we crossed another byroad. Then there was a hollow echo to the wailing and the clack of the wheels on the tracks as we crossed a rusty iron bridge over another large river. Jack, David, and I tossed our last few pieces of gold ore from Colorado overboard into this California gold country river. I wondered if we weren't securing for ourselves, by this act, a golden future. Or did we only do it because it seemed to symbolize the approaching end of our journey? On the train rumbled. There were many more cars on the highway now, and this was reassuring since it seemed to indicate that future transportation would not be a problem.

As we pulled into Stockton, the train slowed as it carefully measured its way along the iron rails. I thought perhaps we would stop at this industrial city, but to my intense pleasure, I felt the train picking up speed once again to continue its race toward the distant smashing waves of the grandest of great oceans.

The scenery maintained its rolling, hilly appearance. The land was covered with dry brown grass waving in the summer breeze. Cattle nuzzled the ground, foraging between clumps of trees for tastier bits of young grass or seed, not in the least alarmed or even disturbed by the roar of our passing train. Even the youngest of the calves, curled in their afternoon naps, slept on undisturbed.

After rolling alongside a small stream lined with shrubs and trees, we entered a short tunnel. The darkness was brief, for we soon emerged at its other end. We continued rolling on toward what seemed to be a large city.

Oakland at last! The track fed through the backstreets of this long-awaited city, heading to its rail yard. Our train slowed more and more as we penetrated deeper into the town. Apparently, the rails ran through the Oakland streets to the yards at the bay end of the city. We all decided there were likely to be many rail police in a yard the size of Oakland. We determined to jump off the slowly moving train onto one of these backstreets now. It would present a danger, of course, to jump from a moving train. It would be easy to lose one's balance and fall under the massive wheels. I warned Jack and Dave and advised them to jump facing the direction in which the train was moving.

"When you get ready to jump, be sure it's from the side of the car," I warned. "The train is moving pretty slow, but you may easily fall."

"Face the direction the train is moving when you release," I repeated.

That way, we wouldn't stop so abruptly, and we could trot more to a stop without losing our balance. They said they understood. We tossed our familiar bedrolls over the side of the gravel car and quickly scrambled down the handrails. I had no trouble with the jump, and Jack too made it safely.

But David was nowhere in sight. I became frightened, fearing the worst. Maybe he hadn't jumped at all. Or maybe he'd fallen under the wheels of the train.

"Jack, you see David?" I yelled.

"No!" he answered. We both looked up and down the railway. Then I saw him releasing the handrail. He had climbed down the car's ladder, which was between cars, fearing he might get separated from us. I nearly swallowed my tongue in my panic. To jump from that ladder would mean he would have to jump at a right angle. That was exactly how he could lose his balance and be crushed between the cars or under those deadly wheels.

As expected, when he jumped, the lumbering car brushed him as it passed, making him lose control of how he would land. However, by luck, its push sent him away from the rails rather than under the wheels. He stumbled and fell in the landing on the street. All he experienced was a skinned knee, but I think my gray hair may have begun to grow then. My feelings raced from fright to wonder to thankfulness to anger. Don had jumped free some time earlier and was now walking toward us. He never saw what happened.

"There he is, Jack," I yelled.

"Yeah, okay," Jack said.

We ran over and helped David to his feet, checking him over. "You okay?" I asked.

"Sure," David answered with a silly grin on his face.

We gathered our gear, Dave explaining that he'd jumped from that ladder as he'd been afraid he would lose us. I thought it best not to say anything further since we were all safe.

Again we wanted to put this city behind us as quickly as possible, always fearing the law would pick us up if we delayed. We were hoboes and looked the part. We not only felt travel-worn and dirty, we were travel-worn and dirty. The soot from the belching smokestack had continually blown back over our open car. We were covered with the sticky mess.

Walking along a side street, we came upon a gas station. Taking care not to be noticed, we made good use of the restroom to get rid of as much of the grime as possible. I imagine the owner wouldn't have been particularly happy had he known that four hoboes were using his bathroom to bathe themselves. Maybe that's why you have to ask them for the key nowadays. In any case, we were happy that at long last our hands and faces were free of the blackness they'd worn for so long. We brushed off our clothes and gear, and then we had a drink of the canned milk left from our meager stores.

Refreshed, we set off to find a highway. This time, we were happy in the knowledge that we were going to be heading south rather than ever west. There was a large lake not far away, a nice-looking lake with green grass growing around it for people to enjoy. We took up our station at a place along the side where a major road passed by. It was only a short wait until an elegant light-blue convertible stopped and picked us up. It surprised me that such a neat-looking driver and vehicle would bother to pick up such obvious bums as us. In this fine car, we sped swiftly down the gray-white concrete of the roadway. It wasn't long before I got my first view of the Pacific Ocean. One goal had been met, and I knew the end was in sight. Within only hours now, we would be in Los Angeles.

Chapter 29

THE HOME STRETCH

When the driver of the convertible dropped us off, we were many miles farther south. A railroad was nearby. It appeared to follow the same path as the highway. A train was sitting on a siding, steam puffing from its engine. We heard the metallic clanging sound it made as it sat in idle. We hurried to investigate and found a long line of oil cars pointing south. They seemed to be waiting for us to climb aboard. We took advantage of this invitation, quickly rushing up the ladder at the end of the car.

Scrambling aboard the nearest oil car, we settled onto one of the long wooden walkways that were located on each side of the car. It was comfortable enough and a reasonably safe place to sit, but it would certainly not do for sleeping had we planned to spend another night on a train.

It seemed that as soon as we were settled, the train—as though it had been waiting for us—gave its familiar lurch. In no time at all we were moving again, traveling California's countryside, heading ever closer to Los Angeles with each click of the wheels on the rails. Sometimes the route brought us within sight of the mighty Pacific. We were awed and refreshed by those thundering waves crashing on the shore. It was a satisfying sight, one our souls had been craving.

The smell of the salt air, together with the sight of the blue-green water filling the world as far as our eyes could see, worked a miracle on our spirits. There were small splashes of white across this great expanse, where wind broke the water into bits of whitecaps several miles out at sea. I could just make out a steamship far out at sea, moving on the horizon to some distant port.

We gazed in fascination at the ocean rising in great slow-motion swells as it worked its way toward the cliffs of the shore. It was the distance that created this deception of slow motion. It was obvious when the waves finally crashed ashore that they had been building and moving with incredible power and speed. Their force against the rocks of the shore sent huge clouds of clean white spray jumping high into the air and tons of water cascading over the rocky formations.

High above all this display of energy, seagulls coasted on the updrafts or plunged into the sea in their hunt for scraps of food. Somehow the birds avoided crashing into one another—a wonder since there were so many of them seemingly paying no attention to one another. We couldn't hear them above the roar of the train, but I knew from experience that the air around them would be filled with their raucous, complaining squawks.

I drank in the California countryside, trying to spot something familiar as we sped past Santa Barbara. We had lived in this area some seven years earlier. It was where Jack and David had been born; but this time, as we watched the hills and towns fly by, we felt like tourists.

Hours passed, and the train was soon slowing for the Los Angeles rail yard. I suddenly found myself afraid. I watched and watched for each new sign that could convince me that we were finally here, that this was truly Los Angeles and the end of the terrible trip. Every building we passed reassured me, providing me more and more evidence that we had indeed arrived in the City of Angels.

Miles of large oil tanks were stacked up near the rail line, tanks storing the black gold of California. The salt smell from the sea was still in our nostrils. I saw the tall buildings of the city looming into view, a grand contrast to the stark ugliness of those left behind in Cincinnati.

Los Angeles had clean whitewashed buildings shining under the sun, compared to the sooty grayness of that hated eastern city. Trees were everywhere, growing green and tall—not stunted into pathetic hopelessness. These California trees surrounded us with a feeling of light, life, and joy—the opposite of the despair we had run from.

It had been so pleasant to roll through the miles of orange groves outside our home city. Now, as this last helpful train applied its brakes, the sound of metal against metal seemed to be a scream of triumph. Almost as though it understood what was in our hearts or was aware of everything we had surmounted in our need to be here.

When the train actually stopped, we gathered our gear for the last time and dropped down to finally put our feet on the soil of Los Angeles. We were safe, and we were home. All we had to do now was to locate our friends in San Pedro, and I knew how to do that. They would know where Mother was.

As we hurried to leave the rail yard, we were suddenly accosted by a security guard. He yelled and cursed at us, saying that he was tired of kids playing around the rail yard. He wasn't going to allow us to get on any of these cars. We heard his continued grumbling over our shoulders as we stepped out of the yard and onto the nearby street.

"Kids these days are headed to no good," he growled.

Jack, David, and I looked at each other, grinning. The guard didn't realize that we weren't leaving.

We had arrived.

1941

Weil Brothers

Jack   David   Bob

Index

Edwards Brothers Malloy
Thorofare, NJ USA
May 27, 2016